PRAISE ✑ **W9-DEB-076**

A Plan for Women

"All is not what it seems in Lawrence Naumoff's fine, un-flinching *A Plan for Women*—a novel both dazzling in its execution and disturbing in its conclusions....Part social comedy, part scathing attack on male dominance, *A Plan for Women* is Naumoff at his finest. In this provocative, unsettling novel, Naumoff has presented his vision with honesty, wit—and something that approaches brilliance."
—*The Miami Herald*

"A provocative novel...When Naumoff exercises his exact-ing sympathy, understanding and humor on the desperate moments of daily life, he brings such compassion to his characters that their struggles are heroically transformed."
—*The New York Times Book Review*

"Laugh-out-loud funny and heart-wrenching, this new novel seductively demands as much self-awareness and honesty from the reader as Naumoff has bravely brought to the page....In *A Plan for Women* Naumoff's finger is not on the pulse of relationships—it's jammed straight into the heart of them—and he holds it there with fearless au-thority."
—*The News & Observer* (Raleigh, NC)

"Naumoff has made a name for himself by exploring male-female relationships and writing in very convincing female voices. In this novel, Naumoff presents his vision of the sexual revolution gone awry. The book is sometimes funny, sometimes wrenching, always provocative."
—*The Charlotte Observer*

"Again combining the notion of women struggling to define themselves against the images of men who would dominate them, Naumoff enriches the mix with a family dynamic that crosses gender and generations.... A thoughtful story...written in a style both crisp and clever."
                                                                    —*Kirkus Reviews*

"Once again, Naumoff's dry eye for anecdotal witness and penchant for dissecting the social anatomy yield a very funny comedy of contemporary manners."
                                                    —*Publishers Weekly* (starred review)

"Naumoff provides plenty of macabre comedy in this odd, disconcerting book about the plans men make for women in the wake of the sexual revolution and the way those plans can come a cropper."
                                                                    —*The Baltimore Sun*

"As engrossing as it is disturbing, Naumoff's latest novel is distinguished by its affectingly precise narrative of women's lives. [He] spins a web of words that is difficult to contemplate without getting caught in its powerful grasp."
                                                                    —*Booklist*

A PLAN
FOR
WOMEN

By Lawrence Naumoff

SILK HOPE, NC

TALLER WOMEN

ROOTIE KAZOOTIE

THE NIGHT OF
THE WEEPING WOMEN

A PLAN FOR WOMEN

LAWRENCE NAUMOFF

A HARVEST BOOK

HARCOURT BRACE & COMPANY

San Diego   New York   London

Copyright © 1997 by Lawrence Naumoff

All rights reserved. No part of this publication
may be reproduced or transmitted in any form or
by any means, electronic or mechanical, including
photocopy, recording, or any information storage
and retrieval system, without permission
in writing from the publisher.

Requests for permission to make copies of
any part of the work should be mailed to:
Permissions Department, Harcourt Brace & Company,
6277 Sea Harbor Drive, Orlando, Florida 32887-6777.

Library of Congress Cataloging-in-Publication Data
Naumoff, Lawrence.
A plan for women/Lawrence Naumoff.—1st ed.
p.   cm.
ISBN 0-15-100231-2
ISBN 0-15-600452-6 (pbk.)
I. Title.
PS3564.A8745P57   1997
813'.54—dc21   97-10951

Text set in Galliard
Designed by Camilla Filancia

Printed in the United States of America
First Harvest edition 1999
A C E D B

*To Marianne
and Michael,
with love.*

Thanks to Kathryn Lindley Davidson
and
Christa Malone
for their help on this book.

SHEOLOGY

Men adored Louise for the pleasure she took in pleasing. Women, it seemed, loved her for what they saw in her heart.

They noticed how eager she was to give herself and they remembered this about their own youth and they sadly wished her well as they watched her sail off into the sea of men around her.

So Louise, a trusting country girl in a clean white nurse's uniform, working in a small town in North Carolina, prim and Southern and well-made, skipped along the surface not knowing exactly what it was about her everyone wanted, not understanding how lucky the man who found her heart would be, simply enjoying life and seducing, in an oddly innocent way, everyone around her—her patients, her family, her friends, and Walter.

Walter's parents, then, would naturally have adored Louise when they met her. His father, especially, was moved to say something to his son he'd been thinking about for some time.

"You know," his father said, "you bring a girl home to meet us."

"Right."

"And then you bring some more."

"I bring more?"

"Yes."

"Louise'll be the last. I'm sure of that."

"And they're all lovely women. All of them."

"Thank you."

"And I look in their eyes and I see how they feel and what they're thinking, and it makes me sad."

"Sad?"

"They're thinking something you're not. It's unfair, Walter. It's simply unfair."

"I don't know what you mean."

"Yes you do."

"What's your point, Dad? Make your point."

"My point is this. Stop. Stop whatever it is you're doing with these girls. It's not right."

"Not right?"

"Just leave them be."

Walter's father was eighty-six years old. He had practiced medicine until he was eighty-four. He was an old man who had married late in his life and conceived his son even later. After all these years, he still did not know Walter.

"I treasure Louise," Walter said. "I would never hurt her."

The visit soon ended. It was just after supper on a summer evening in Charlotte, North Carolina.

The house the young couple left, the house where Walter had grown up, was spacious but modest and represented the dignity and lack of ostentation that physicians in the South from his father's generation thought proper. Few doctors whose practices had begun to thrive in the late forties or early fifties bought Cadillacs when they finally could. They bought Pontiacs or Buicks. The idea of flaunting one's wealth didn't suit good Southern physicians back then. Modesty and a virtuous life and a dignified presentation of one's self and good works for mankind had been mandated for Walter. It hadn't always been easy to live up to all of that.

"You're not happy?" Louise asked as they drove home.

"I'm happy," he said. "I'm happy to be with you."

On the way home to Chapel Hill, Walter took Louise to a drive-in outside of town. She'd never been to one, which seemed right because he was older than she and had done many things that she had not.

Louise was high as a kite after spending all day with Walter. She was keeping herself in check, though, and holding back from talking about anything and everything that was rushing into her mind, trying to be dignified and quiet, like he was. Had she let herself go, her words would have popped out of her mouth like stars from a sparkler and lit up the night sky all around them.

To Louise, Walter was such an interesting man, an absolute wonder. The men her own age were dull, predictable jerks. Walter treated her well and made her laugh and took her seriously. As they settled down to watch the movie, which was about a woman who was betrayed by a man who wrote a song about her and became famous while she became infamous, she studied his face and desired him in every way.

Soon she noticed Walter watching not the movie but the car beside them, where a man, a woman, and an unusually tiny child were in the front seat.

"What's going on?" she asked, unable to see into the car as well as he.

Walter watched the woman take the child from an infant seat and put it on her lap. As she did, he realized it was, in fact, a rubber doll dressed up like a boy, wearing a cap on its painted-hair rubber head and a homemade suit-jacket and pants.

"Something weird," he said.

As they watched, the man reached for the doll. The woman pulled it away and he missed. He lunged for it again and this time he got it. He tossed it onto the backseat and then pinned the woman's arms so she couldn't reach it. She began to cry.

"Oh, Lord," Louise said.

The man held the woman's arms firmly and shook his head no as she pleaded with him. He pointed to the screen, and after a minute or so they began watching the movie again.

"That's awful," Louise said.

"I can't exactly figure that out."

Then, while the woman was staring ahead at the screen, the man eased his arm into the backseat and quietly dropped the little doll out the open window. He seemed unsettled after that. Soon he started the car and they drove off.

In the empty space where the car had been was the doll. It did, on first glance, look like a miniature human child. Lying in the dust with its painted, parted lips open against the dirt and its hat a few feet away and its tiny homemade little-man suit askew, it was more curious than what was on the screen.

"Put your arm around me," Louise said. "I feel sad from that."

A mother and daughter passed the doll. The daughter, who was holding her mother's hand, pulled away and picked up the doll. The mother watched her child brush off the dirt, pick up the hat, and put it on the doll's head. The little leather-like moccasins that had been made for this doll were hanging loose, and the girl put them back in place, as well, then offered the doll to her mother.

Her mother set the doll back on the ground, looking around to see if anyone would claim it. Then they walked on.

"She should've taken it," Louise said.

"I don't know. Maybe not."

"Yeah. Maybe not."

She snuggled under his arm. He hadn't held her all day. They'd been too busy with too many people.

"What an odd thing to have seen," she said. "And after such a day."

It had been odd to Walter, as well. He thought, though, without saying it, that it was simply another moment in the lives of women that was as sad as it was bizarre.

The young woman beside him was not yet sad or bizarre or defeated or depressed or enraged or crazed. This was the gift of young women, although often their cherished, light-headed beliefs would eventually fail when abutting the impurity and the solitary demands of certain men they would meet. Things would change. For these women, then, who had the gift of trust and the purity of their beliefs, betrayal was nearby. Sadness and longing were not far behind.

"Can I ask you something?" Louise said.

"Sure."

"How come we've been together all these months and you've never wanted to sleep with me?"

There was, in the actions of a woman who would cry over a doll, who would have her arm mashed into the seat to keep her still, who would be forced to watch a screen where people read lines and pretended to be who they weren't, there was in the knowledge of that woman's existence and in women like her, in the knowledge of what had gone before and what was to come, a question for any man who loved a woman that had to be answered.

"Don't you want to?" Louise asked.

CHAPTER 3

LOUISE'S MOTHER and father lived outside of
Chapel Hill in an area that had once been rural. Their two
acres were now surrounded by townhomes and develop-
ments. When the visual canvas of the South had been repainted by the invention of the condominium, spacious
lawns and the graciousness of privacy had disappeared
along with cheap land.

"Dar? Where are you?"

Dorothy, Louise's mother, was in the attic, and below,
in the well-laid-out, single-story spread of rooms, her husband, Vincent, was looking for her. They had been married
thirty-four years and Louise was their only child, coming
after three miscarriages.

"Are you in the bathroom?" Vincent called.

Louise, who was twenty-one, had moved out of the
house this year. Dorothy missed her not only because
they were good friends but because she and Vincent were
not—though this in itself was not unusual in the marriages
of the women she knew.

"Are you in the attic again?"

Because it was the weekend and because she knew
Vincent would ask her to help him with this or that project
and because she knew when she did she would end up

getting pinched or mashed or yelled at, she had been in the attic for two hours, sorting through clothes, reminiscing about Louise, and hoping that being out of sight would save her.

"You are up there," he said from the bottom of the pull-down stairway. "Would you mind coming down?"

When she rose, her head bumped the underside of the rafters and a hair wound around a splinter and held her tight.

Oh. Ow, ow, ow, she said to herself as she tried to pull loose the hair.

"I just need you for a few minutes," Vincent said.

Oh God, it hurts, she thought as the hair came loose, not from the splinter but from her scalp.

Dorothy came down the stairway backward, holding the rails and facing the giant green painted blades of the old attic fan, another relic of times past, having been replaced by the central air conditioning.

"Let me change into something else," she told Vincent. She closed her bedroom door while he waited in the hall, pacing.

She put on slacks, a blouse, and a pair of simple flats. She was one of those women who would never own a pair of jeans or tennis shoes. For her generation and for her parents' generation, jeans were so strictly associated with working class people that it was unthinkable to wear them, even now. It would have been like admitting her family or ancestors were coal miners or farmers.

"Bounce the car up and down," Vincent said.
"I can't."
"Try it."
"I'm trying, but I can't," she said.

"Well, then hold the wrench right there and I'll do it."

"I can't reach in there."

"Why, Dar? Why can't you reach in there?"

"Because my hair'll get dirty."

"Then bounce the car up and down."

"I'm just not heavy enough."

He huffed over to his car and took a cap from the front seat. The cap said NAPA AUTO PARTS.

"I'm not wearing that."

"Just put it on. It'll keep your hair clean."

"I will not wear that hat."

"Then don't complain about your hair."

"I'm not complaining. I'm stating a fact."

"Do you want your car fixed or not?"

"I want it fixed. I just don't want to be the one who does it," she said.

"You have to make everything harder than it is," he said. "You just have to."

"No, I don't have to. I don't intend to," she said. "Give me the wrench," she told him, deciding to go numb and do whatever it was she had to do.

On the first full travel downward of the car on its shock absorbers, Dorothy's fingers were pinched between the underside of the fender and the wrench. When the car rose up, she pulled her hand away and dropped the wrench, at the same time making a noise like a bird chirping, but with its beak held closed.

I knew it, she said to herself. I knew it, I knew it, I knew it.

"What happened?"

"You mashed my hand."

"I'm sorry. Listen, change places with me. We'll find a way."

He stuck his head between the fender and tire while

she leaned on the fender and bounced the car up and down.

"Is that where you heard the noise?" he asked.

"I guess."

"Or here?" he asked, pointing close by.

"I think so."

"Can you be a little more precise? I need the more-or-less, I-guess, sort-of, I-think-but-I'm-not-sure spot."

"Here."

"All right. Now we're getting somewhere. Get up on the car and simulate it bouncing like it would be if we're moving. Do it hard."

She first leaned on the hood and then, when she wasn't able to give it enough force, climbed all the way up.

"How about that?" she asked.

"I can't quite hear it the way you described it. I'm not saying you imagined it. I just can't hear anything."

Vincent quickly went to the driver's side and started the engine. She looked at him through the windshield as he lowered the passenger side window and leaned over.

"I'm going to roll along kind of slow, and you make it like we're on a bumpy road," he said.

"Wait a minute."

"I want to hear it from inside. I think you're hearing something from somewhere else. I've got to isolate it without the traffic noise."

He put the window up and started rolling around the house, driving across the lawn. Dorothy held to the wiper arm with one hand and flattened herself against the fender with the other.

"Bounce," he said.

"What?"

"Bounce," he yelled and moved his hand up and down in a spanking motion. "Bounce it."

The squeak then began, but it was faint.

"Good. More."

He went around the yard faster. He traveled through the front yard, up the side, across the back, and then around again, dodging the flower beds and boxwoods and dogwoods and the big magnolia tree. He rolled down the window on his side and leaned his head out to hear it better. Concentrating along the driver's side of the car and looking just in front of that side to guide himself, he failed to notice that his wife was now sliding around on the hood.

"Good," he yelled when he glanced at her, thinking she'd really put her heart into it. "That way's even better."

He made a few more trips around the yard while Dorothy lay face forward and off center like a comically askew and bizarre hood ornament, or a dead deer laid out for everyone to see.

"Terrific. You did great," he said after he parked. He flew around to the back of the car and stuck his head underneath. "That was even better lying over like that."

Dorothy oozed off the hood and onto her hands and knees.

"I've got it," he called out triumphantly. "It's a heat shield."

There, she thought. It's over. Pray the rest of the weekend will be uneventful. Pray Louise will swing by for a visit. Pray that nothing else inside the house or on the car or in the yard will ever break again, that nothing will have to be moved or loaded or carried. Pray that Louise will be able to say no, that nothing will go so wrong in her life. Pray that she will not find herself in a situation where she can never say no to a man, that she will not find herself in the position of her own mother who, it seemed, could not use that word.

CHAPTER 4

SOME CHILDREN had stable childhoods with parents who stayed together and prospered. Others had parents who remarried a half-dozen times, losing at each divorce more and more to the ex-husbands and ex-wives.

The fortunate children, whose families remained together and also prospered, now had a financial security that had the power to make life easier. At the same time, money badly spent could ruin life. Ending up with that much money early on, or simply knowing it was there, meant that those privileged children could purchase anything they wanted, from drugs to cars to houses to, as often as not, other people.

There were, then, in Walter's generation, men and women like Mary Pristine Calhoun who found that as they got older and made more mistakes and became more confused, rather than less, all the answers, or at least the only ones they could find, revolved around loneliness, sexuality, and desire.

In the case of Mary Pristine, her life centered around men, and though she was educated enough to know that was wrong, she could not seem to correct it.

She was thirty-six years old, dark-haired, and her ancestors were Welsh, Irish, English, and German. She watched what she ate and, when she wasn't depressed or hung over, took walks in the morning and even jogged a few blocks now and again.

"You're going to have fun with me," she said.

The man she was talking to, and with whom she'd gone to the party, was an instructor in English at the local college.

"I can do it twice," she whispered to him. "More, sometimes."

They were standing under a willow tree. Mary had been drinking since before Rob even picked her up.

"I like to be on top," she said and pulled him to her and began to kiss him. "I'm good at it that way."

She was crazy to get him back to her house. She hadn't had sex in three months.

"I like to make a lot of noise," she whispered. "It makes it better."

He grabbed a branch from the tree to keep his balance as Mary Pristine pushed herself into him while kissing him and whispering in his ear.

"Let's go across the creek," she said.

The party was in the backyard of one of Mary's friends. A creek ran behind the property. Along this creek was a row of weeping willows whose branches arched down to the ground and whose tiny leaves came off in her hand like green confetti.

"I want to eat you up, mister," she said. "You'll never forget this night the rest of your life."

Two children rode bicycles with raised handlebars. They rolled past Mary and Rob and around the other people at the party and under the willows, and as they passed Mary Pristine, she stuck her hand out and tagged each one of them, dreamily.

"Children are nice," she said.

They rode into the shallow creek and up the other bank and then back into the party. The tires had no fenders, and the spray of water made dark lines down the spines of both children. Neither the little girl nor the boy wore a shirt. At that age, the difference between them wasn't immediately apparent. It seemed a nice thing, that they were the same.

"Do you have any children?" she asked, and dropped her hand down his side and into his pants pocket.

Two black boys about nine or ten years old were prying open oysters. Years ago, all across the South, young Negro boys stood by tables in fish houses cracking oysters throughout the night for a couple of dollars in tips. For white natives of the area, the sight of these boys was a fondly nostalgic memory of the way things used to be, as much as would have been coming upon an old Negro man mowing your grass, who might doff his cap and call you Cap'n and then later you look out the window and see him sitting at the picnic table in the backyard, eating watermelon with the maid.

Seeing that, you knew you were going to give them both one heck of a Christmas gift and, eventually, the family Oldsmobile when you were finished with it.

"Do you want to take a walk? Do you want to leave? Just tell me what you want," Mary Pristine said.

The oysters were being served three ways: breaded and deep-fried or raw or steamed in the shell and popped straight into your mouth. The boys would set them up any way you wanted them.

"Are you hungry?" she asked.

Some people were dancing. A Jimmy Buffet song was coming from the speakers. It was a lazy summer evening in the South, and Mary's bare shoulders were glistening with perspiration. Drops of sweat trickled down under her arms and along the back of her neck beneath her hair.

"Do you want another gin and tonic?"

A thirty-gallon garbage can for the empty oyster shells was beside the table where the boys were at work. Along the coast oyster shells had been crushed and used as gravel on driveways and parking lots for years. Walking barefoot on this blend of finely crushed shells felt strange and unlike anything else you'd ever walked barefoot on. Some of the pieces could be sharp. Children from inland might not know this and might run headlong across the gray and white sandy expanse, only to jump into the air with a piece of shell stuck in their foot.

"Do you dance? Do you want to now?"

Barefoot on the finely ground parts of the shells felt wonderful. It was sensuous, and women especially liked this warm, grainy, and resilient feeling against their feet. Women and children seemed to like it the most.

"Raw oysters don't do a thing for me," Mary said.

The children had parked their bikes and were sitting side by side on the ground. The boy had a blade of grass between his thumbs and was teaching the girl how to blow it like a reed so that it made the sound of a screeching clarinet. The little girl was thrilled by this new trick.

"I want another G and T. I don't care what anyone says."

The little girl's face glowed when she succeeded in blowing across the blade of grass and making the sound. Both of them found new blades and began to work at making them screech. It was a lovely sight, and made everyone at the party feel good.

"My ex-therapist asked me not to drink for six months," Mary said. She was standing side by side with Rob now and holding his hand with one of hers and moving it around on her neck, giving herself the chills almost as if he'd been doing it by himself. "At my age, six months is a long time."

One of the parents noticed that the shuckers had finished with the oysters and that they were waiting at the edge of the party with nothing to do. The parent approached the boy who was blowing on the reed of grass and spoke to him. Soon he and the girl wheeled their bicycles over to the shuckers and offered to let them ride.

"Rub me here," Mary said. "It feels really nice there."

The two black boys began doing wheelies, riding on the back tire with the front one up in the air. The boys were covered with splatter and grime from opening the shells, and one of them had a raised scar running from above his eyebrow into his cheek.

"I can't do without anything," Mary said. "After a while you realize you can't."

For a moment, when the little girl was getting her bicycle back from the boy, it looked like a scene from a Shirley Temple movie, with the friendly child from the big house having a little fun with the slave-quarter children.

"Let's go skinny-dipping somewhere," Mary said.

The maid who was carrying the dishes in and out of the house put the two boys to work carrying what was left of the food and drink. The party was over. Everyone was going home.

"How about it?" Mary Pristine asked. "Or are you chicken."

Someone's car had backed into a wet spot and was stuck. The people remaining helped push it out. It seemed really funny, the car getting stuck and people falling down and getting mud splattered all over their clothes as they pushed it out. Everyone was laughing as hard as they could.

The two black boys were watching at the kitchen window. The expressions on their faces had not changed during the entire night. Not when they were working, not when they were doing wheelies, and not now, as they watched the white people pushing the car and getting hysterical about it.

"You drive," Mary Pristine said. "I'm too damn drunk to care whether I stay on the road or not."

They went into Mary's house, and she took off her clothes and got into bed. Rob was in the bathroom. When he came out, she closed her eyes and looked away. She hated herself. She wished she were anywhere but there at that moment.

He pulled down the sheet and put his hand between her legs.

"When you get through with it, just cover it back up," she said and turned her face to the wall and tried not to scream from the waste and suffocating hell she had made of her life.

CHAPTER 5

NEXT TO Walter's home were three houses that had been built by Homes for Humanity, the organization that Walter directed. Wanting to make a statement about the need for such housing in all neighborhoods, he had sold, at well below market value, the three lots for these houses. His neighbors, already annoyed with Walter's own experimentally designed house in their traditional neighborhood, had not been happy about this sale.

It was the right thing for Walter to help people, to be generous, to be open-minded, to be fearless in the defense of weaker and easily exploited people, to set himself against the forces that craftily orchestrated the beliefs and designs of modern life.

The predatory nature of commerce had become so scientifically thorough and, at the same time, so cunningly able to exploit human weakness and desire for commercial gain that it was the mandate of any strong individual to take a stand against this kind of power, even if it was merely on the personal level of helping people to understand that three houses would not harm their lives.

In the house closest to Walter's own home, which was separated from his by their side yards and plantings, a woman sat up alone in bed. She did not know she would be alone when she awoke in this new house, which though simple and relatively small was the nicest one she'd ever lived in.

It had a south-facing clerestory wall that created, on the interior, a modest cathedral-ceilinged family room. The rest of the house was single story, with vinyl formed to resemble lapped wooden siding, aluminum-framed double-paned windows, a front porch, and a back deck. The railings and pickets around the porch and deck conformed to local standards, which allowed for no more than three inches in the clear between each single picket. This dimension had been arrived at so that neither children nor babies could get their heads caught in between the pickets and die.

Shirley Tisdale did not want to die. Since she'd been with Manny, she hadn't thought of it. Now, in this lovely home, it was as remote as the names of the other men she'd met, as remote as the places she'd known them.

Manny was good to her. He had only hit her twice and only one of those times in the face. Of those two total times, she thought she actually deserved it once, so that, all in all, having been hit twice in three months, and one of those times being her own fault, this was another lucky woman, who, like Louise, had found a good man.

Shirley knew from the first day that Manny was good because he literally saved her life, an act for which she owed him, however long it took to repay.

The night she first saw him, he and one of his friends kidnapped her from the parking lot of a convenience store. Manny and his buddy had been planning to rape her, but when they stopped on a dirt road and put her on the ground, he saw what a nice girl she was and prevented his friend from doing anything.

He let her ride home in the front seat with them, even though his friend was mad and cussed her out the whole time. In the car he and Shirley got to know each other and agreed to meet later in the week.

She'd been right. Except for those two times, one of which didn't count, Manny had been good to her and had already held four jobs since they'd been together. As soon as he was let go from one, he got another, making good on the promise he'd take care of her.

Not only that, but when social services allowed Shirley's daughter to visit them overnight, Manny had been as nice and caring as if she had been his own daughter, which, if looks counted, she might have been, since she was half black due to her father being black, and since Manny himself was half black. It all almost fit.

He was good with the house, too. That was important because it belonged to Shirley's sister and her husband, who had qualified for the subsidy and assistance. Shirley was just looking after it until her sister and brother-in-law got out of jail.

She loved being home, and Manny was trying to get her to quit her cashier's job now that she was pregnant.

She was still in bed late that morning. Though they had made love twice the night before, she wanted to do it again in the morning, being fairly sure that if she had him before he went to work, he wouldn't cheat on her while he was away.

It was eleven-thirty. She was hungry. She should eat something. The house had a nice kitchen. Maybe soon Manny would give her some money for groceries. Maybe she would ask him for some, if he was in a good mood when he got home.

She looked in the mirror. She didn't like what she saw. Maybe Manny didn't either.

CHAPTER 6

WHY WAS IT, Walter thought, that the faces of women seemed changed? More glamorous than ever, they seemed, at the same time, sad and degraded, as if the women had only recently discovered something terrible, as if these women were refugees from a long war, with black-and-white ghostly overlays that made them seem out of focus.

"I'll just have a half a sandwich," he said.

Beneath the glamour of the vibrant, tawny skin framed by the mane of richly colored hair remained the pale, melancholy specter of someone else, meager and gossamer like a hungry, war-orphaned child.

"A ginger ale to drink, also," he said.

In the case of older women, the duplicity of their pleasures, which was contained like holograms in their lips and eyes and sunken cheeks, became something different altogether. What remained in their faces was, oddly enough, more defined and truthful than what had been before, as if in aging, the false skin had been shed.

"Any kind of bread will do. Rye, I guess."

In a young woman, the ripe offering of all the promises made to men parted the yearning lips while the eyes closed, as if in dream.

"That'll be all."

Louise's face was clear and perfect and bright. She had a purity and strength beneath her chatty Southern femininity that made her attractive to Walter in a way no other woman had ever been.

Across the large open room of the delicatessen sat a woman about Louise's age. She had a nice face. A man could easily love a woman for what he saw in her face, but it would be a reckless thing to do. Being reckless felt good, but only briefly.

The woman across the room, who had a nice face but was not Louise in any way to Walter, was eating alone. Eating alone in restaurants was something that women didn't do very often. If they did, they took a book or some papers from work. Merely sitting alone and digging hungrily into a plate of food didn't seem right for women, who would be publicly revealing appetite and desire.

Desire was something that, until recently, women were supposed to keep secret.

Walter's belief that this would have been a secret, and his image of the prim woman who was clean and pure and the guardian of moral goodness and excess, came from the women in his life, his mother and his sister as a young girl. It came from their calm posture in a chair, with the legs tucked neatly together and to one side, with their hands in their laps as still as sleeping kittens.

The woman across the cafe was neither prim nor still. She ate as if she were starved and drank her spring water right out of the bottle, ignoring the cup the waitress brought and sucking the water out of the bottle as if she were abnormally dry.

She bit her sandwich as if she were mad at it and ate her potato chips with the same vigor, so that wayward particles shattered into the air and onto the table and across the neatly fitted bodice of her blouse.

As Walter watched her, he realized he was taking tiny

bites of his own sandwich and eating with the deliberation and modesty of a woman, or at least in the manner he had always considered female. This is curious, he thought, as if he were making up for the woman's abandon.

The woman left. Ten minutes later Walter paid his check, tucked two one-dollar bills neatly under his coffee cup for the tip, and walked five blocks to wait for Louise in front of the theater.

He saw her park her car. When she saw him, she ran.

"Hey," she said and kissed him. "I know I'm late. That's why I said go ahead and eat without me. I knew I would barely get away in time to get cleaned up and meet you here. I'm sorry."

"You be as late as you want," he said. "It's you I'm waiting for, not the movie."

"Let's go in. I'll tell you about my day later. What a day."

"You look lovely, by the way."

"I don't. I don't see how I could. I feel like a wreck."

"You look like an angel."

"You need glasses," she said.

"Actually," he told her and put his hands on both sides of her face and made her slow down and look at him, "you are an angel. You truly are."

This was something she wanted to believe, not that she actually was, but that he thought she was. She wanted to be. Somehow he made her want to be as good as he believed she was, even if she couldn't believe it herself, even if she knew it wasn't true.

At the same time Walter had been eating his supper and Louise had been rushing home to change, her parents were finishing their meal and getting ready for the evening news.

It was six twenty-five, and they always finished supper and came into the den at this time.

"You know, it's no big deal how you cut up the beans and cooked them," Vincent said, "but it's just that I'm used to them a certain way."

"If it's no big deal, then forget it."

"I mean to say, you've cut them up in little pieces for years now. I just didn't expect it."

"All right. I get it."

"They're called snap beans. I know that. But when you snap them, they cook different."

"Okay," Dorothy said.

"I mean, words are just words."

"I got it, Vincent. I won't do it again."

"I mean, black folks are all kinds of colors. White folks aren't white, not really white, like chalk."

"You're right."

"Black-eyed peas can't see."

"True."

"Big Boy tomatoes ain't boys."

"No, they're not boys, Vincent."

"Here comes the news. Are you going to watch it with me, or what?"

She was stuck on this one. She tried to figure out if he meant he wanted her to, or not.

"Or are you going to clean up in there."

"I'll clean up."

Sometimes, when a man comes home from work, he's tired, and things could have happened during his day that a placid, content, and relaxed homemaker of a wife might never guess could happen. A lot of things a man says when he first gets home, he doesn't mean, and usually, after he's fed he feels better, unless something on the news gets him upset again and then he might talk about it all night until bedtime when he falls dead asleep because he's had a hard day and he's tired and men die at a younger age than women and then sometimes a woman is left all alone, to think about things, or to start her life all over again.

MARY LONGED for excitement of almost any kind, though none seemed in sight.

She took in the mail. In it were envelopes from banks and brokers and various funds, and inside them were the statements of what was called the activity of her money.

These figures meant nothing to her, nothing at all. Even the final balance was often just a small-print number with commas and zeros separating six, seven, or eight digits, including the cents.

That the digits to the right of the decimal point were included annoyed her. Why would anyone care whether they had 4 cents or 31 cents along with 467,893 dollars, or whatever the amount was on a particular statement? How could it matter?

"Doctor Mullet? This is Mary P. Calhoun," she said, leaving a message on the answering machine. "Call me as soon as you can. Thanks."

Outside, a crew of women from a halfway house was mowing and trimming and raking her yard.

It hadn't been that many years since she'd done that work herself, when she'd been married to Harris Benjamin Calhoun, who had been, at least more than anyone else, the love of her life.

It hadn't been that many years since she had seen him on their porch, drinking gin and tonics on cool fall afternoons while she raked leaves from the oaks and maples.

She had been thrilled to have him there, to be able to see him taking it easy while she worked. The idea of this happy satisfied man at home with her, relaxed with her, pleased with her, delighted by her, was so absurdly simple and easy and comfortable that, in the end, she had to mess it up. She had to get herself agitated over what she wasn't and what he wasn't and what she didn't have and who she didn't have and all of it somehow connected with this general feeling of not being fulfilled, of having lost her sexy, bright, and quick edge.

The women in the yard were young. They were strong. They had made their own mistakes. They were paying for their mistakes in a way she herself had not. Theirs were different kinds of errors. When they finished paying, the penance would all be over.

The women were taking good care of Mary's yard. She had a nice house in an excellent older section of town. Her neighbors had husbands and children. The ones in the big house directly across the street had grown children and grandkids who came to visit and ran wildly around all over the neighborhood, as she had done, herself, as a child.

It was six-forty in the evening. The women had worked late. Working hard like that might be fun. It might feel good.

"Doctor Mullet? This is Mary Calhoun again. Call me soon, will you? Call me tonight, if you can."

The phone rang within a minute of that call. She turned her head so fast the ash on the end of her cigarette fell into her lap.

"Oh, hi," she said. "No. Thanks, but no. I don't feel like it. Not really. I just don't feel too particularly energetic, you know? Call me another time."

It was Rob, the man she'd been out with the night of the oyster party. He kept talking to her. He talked a long time.

"I know. You're right. I ought to get out. I do need to get out. You're right about that. I guess so. I'll be ready. Yeah. Thanks for calling."

Vaguely, she did not want to go out with him. Vaguely, she did. She could not clearly recall much about the other night.

She could remember, though, that it was sometimes easier to have sex with a man than to say his name, that it was easier to go ahead and get into bed and do it than to actually look at him and call his name.

She could remember how sweet it was when a man she loved made her come like she wanted to, how absolutely divine it was to go so far she almost couldn't get back, to let him turn her into spun sugar so that she felt more like cotton candy than skin and bones. She could remember that.

She just couldn't remember how to get there anymore. Maybe it started with being able to look a man in the eye and say his name.

CHAPTER 8

BEFORE LOUISE decided to move in with her friend and co-worker Nancy, she observed that her childhood seemed to have become prolonged not only by the never-changing and maddening drama of her father and mother but by her desire to be there for her mother, by her desire not to leave home. Leaving home was, in a sense, abandoning her mother to Vincent.

"You call me every day," she had told her mother, "and I'll call you every day."

Oddly, though they had always talked as friends, she had never heard her mother admit how discouraging life was married to Vincent. Louise wasn't sure whether her mother didn't think her life was as bad as it was or whether she just wouldn't admit that it was bad.

"I'll never have a man who won't talk to me," Louise had told her mother. "Daddy never says a word to you except bring me this, bring me that, do this, do that."

"It's hard to explain, honey," her mother had said. "There are reasons why things are the way they are. I guess they're good reasons."

"You'll never see me marry unless my husband's my best friend and always will be. I won't have it any other way."

"Things start out fine," her mother had said. "Usually, they do for everyone. I hope you find all of that. I think you will."

Now, having a good man who would be her friend and would respect her seemed real and not merely bold words.

Living with Nancy, then, if she did not count the few strictly and truly from-hell months she had lived with someone else, which she was determined to forget, was Louise's first actual home away from home.

She and Nancy worked together in the hospital in the same department. They were good friends to the point of knowing all about each other, including Louise's months in hell.

"Because Walter wants to marry me," she was telling Nancy, "the day's coming when he's got to meet my parents. As much as I hate the thought of it, it's going to happen. He's bound to think less of me once he meets my dad."

"It's really sudden," Nancy said.

"No, it's not."

"There's so much to consider."

They were taking a walk and were going at it so hard they talked breathlessly and loudly.

"I've considered it all."

"Let's see," Nancy said, "fill in the blanks. He'll be blank when I'm blank."

"Yeah, yeah, yeah. When I'm forty, he'll be fifty-nine."

"And don't get mad at me for saying this, but it's odd he's never been married. Most men have by that age."

"He never wanted to marry anyone until he met me."

"Uh huh."

"I believe him. We are so right together. Don't you think I'd be careful after what I've been through?"

"Yeah, you would. I'm just asking questions. Do you like his family, by the way? That's important."

"I love them. I haven't met his sister, but I've heard about her."

"What's her name?"

"I can't remember. It seems like he told me, but I can't remember."

"Where does she live?"

"Oh, Lord. Is this a sign things really are moving too fast."

"It might be."

A bus approached the bench where they had decided to rest. Louise waved it on, but it slowed anyway.

"Can't that fool see me waving him off?" Louise asked.

She waved her hand like a cop trying to get the traffic to move on through, to hurry up.

"Gosh durned idiot," she said. "Man, can't you see we're not waiting for you?"

The bus stopped. Two people departed from the back entrance. Then it drove away.

"I'm losing it," Louise said. "Do you want to know something?"

"Sure."

"I've been trying not to say anything about it, but I want to tell you."

"Tell me."

"Do you know that we want to marry each other, that we're madly in love, that we're together practically all the time, and when we kiss I just about come apart at the seams, and yet he won't make love with me."

"You've got to be kidding? You haven't done it?"

"No. All he'll do is kiss me. Nothing else. I mean, nothing else."

"Weird. Maybe too weird."

"I put his hands on my breasts the other night and

rubbed them on me, and he kissed me and said later, sweetheart, later."

"I don't like the sound of this," Nancy said.

"What does it mean?"

"I don't know."

"He seems worried about it."

"Louise, if you were me and I were you, I'd be sure he
could do it before we got married. What if he can't?"

"I've thought about that. Wouldn't you be supposed
to go ahead and marry him, even if he couldn't? If you
loved a man?"

"I don't think so."

"I do. I think you would."

"Let's walk some more," Nancy said. "And talk about
this."

"You know, it's like he's got some plan. It seems that
way. It's kind of nice, if you want to know the truth.
There's something really sexy about it."

"I doubt it."

"There is. I don't know what it is, but there's something about the way he's doing with me that gets to me.
I don't know what it is."

Most of the two acres that Louise's parents owned
around their house was in the back. Around the border of
the yard were flower beds and fruit trees. The trees were
now mature and productive, and it was the fruit from one
of the cherry trees that she had gathered after the birds had
finished with their share that Dorothy used for a pie that
was now cooling on a wire rack.

"I hope he don't like that pie," Vincent said.

"I hope he does," Dorothy said, "And don't say *don't*
like that. You know better."

"I don't know nothing."

"Please behave."

"I'd behave better if you'd make pies like that for me."

"All you've got to do is ask," she said.

"And all you got to do is make one. Just make it, anytime, and I'll eat it."

Louise parked in front of Walter's house.

I could live here, she thought. It's odd, it's weird, but I could do it, she told herself, studying the design.

The house had two round sections connected by a rectangular passage. One section was larger than the other. Both had an abundance of glass, which had been custom manufactured and curved for this particular house. To Louise, and to many other people, the structure looked like something from an amusement park.

"It was great on paper," Walter had told her when she first saw it. "You wouldn't believe how good it looked on the plans."

"It's really interesting," she had said.

"Then, after I built it, well, there it was. I don't know what happened. I planned it out all so carefully, and then it didn't work."

In the front yard, where you would expect some grass, was a vegetable garden overrun with wildflowers and weeds. Louise was picking some flowers when Walter came out.

"You won't need those," he said. "About now, the florist should be delivering an arrangement to your parents' house."

That touched her so she wanted to cry and laugh all at once. Every day he proved how absolutely different he was from any other man she'd ever known, from any boy she'd ever dated.

"You didn't have to do that," she said.

"And I've got a box of cigars for your dad. They're almost Havana. They're from the same stock and grown by the same families that used to make them in Cuba. They're three dollars apiece."

"You bought him a whole box?"

"I'm covering my bases. They may not like me. They may not like the age difference. Who knows what they'll think of me."

"Who knows what you'll think of them. That's the story there," she said.

Once, in a film, Hulk Hogan had to care for some children. He didn't know what he was doing. He was a wrestler. He didn't understand the concept of home and family and children. Sometimes, in the film, people's heads crashed through walls, appearing on the other side like targets at the fair.

Dorothy had watched the movie on television and, in her generous-hearted, simple way, had understood her husband better. The revelation had not come from the study of religion, though she was a churchgoing person, or from a study of the great thinkers of times past but from a made-for-TV movie about Hulk Hogan.

She had thought a lot about it after seeing it, and it had made her more forgiving of her husband. He had never actually realized what a self-centered and crude man he'd been in his life because she had never told him, and she had never told him because he wouldn't have understood what she was talking about and because she owed him whatever it took.

"Take your time," she said, seeing him gorging on the hors d'oeuvres she had set out. "We have all night."

"I don't get stuff like this ever. Damn if you aren't putting on the show for this boy."

"Leave some for Walter and Louise. Please."

He ate while standing up, going from one tray to another. As he left one, Dorothy hurried to it and rearranged what was left.

CHAPTER 9

THE MOTEL where Mary and Rob went was on Highway 70 between Durham and Hillsborough. Not many travelers used that road anymore.

"We could've gone back to my house," she said.

Not many people used the motel anymore, either. The room smelled as if it hadn't been opened in weeks. The air conditioner had been on for only ten minutes when a line of water began to drip from the bottom.

"Or yours," she said. "But you wanted to come here?"

The air conditioner had been improperly installed so that it slanted back into the room rather than toward the outside. The water dripped steadily.

"I guess you're right. This place is campy, and retro. That's the oldest TV I've ever seen in a motel. I bet it's black and white," she said.

The ceiling tiles above the bed where Mary sat were loose. When a person looks directly upward, directly and sharply above him or her, the mouth is drawn open by the muscles in the neck pulling the lower jaw downward.

"Is this place, like, intentionally retro, just as is?" she asked.

If a person heard a scratching sound and looked upward and one of the tiles came loose above her, dirt and little bugs of all kinds might fall into her mouth and crawl around on her tongue trying to get out. That would be something a person would be unlikely to forget.

"Let's see if the TV works," she said. "And give me that bottle. And get me some ice."

Most of these old motels were constructed with hollow cinder blocks set on low concrete slabs.

"Look at that ashtray with the map of North Carolina on it. Damn. This is a time warp. I'm in the third grade and we're traveling to Gettysburg to see what the Yankees did to us."

Carpet was glued to the slab. Sometimes after a rain a person could walk barefoot over the carpet and feel where the water had been absorbed from below into the dry foam backing. Sometimes after a big rain, if a person shone the gooseneck lamp beside the bed close to the rug, she might see silverfish swimming around. Their phosphorescent bodies would glisten like slivers of foil among the nylon fibers. The whole rug would seem to be moving.

"That was a great movie we saw. Someone ought to make a movie about my life."

A piece of fried chicken was under the bed. It had been there for weeks. If a woman were lying on the bed on her stomach because someone had asked her to lie that way, she might see the little chicken bone peeping out from under the bed. That would not be the romantic vision she would have been hoping for.

"What's in the bag?"

Sometimes men, especially those in their fifties and sixties, need props to get aroused. There was nothing new about this and women had abstracted the act ever since they first started doing it.

"You're joking, right?"

One time a man got angry at a woman because she

closed her eyes when he had asked her not to. He was angry because he knew she wasn't thinking about him at that moment. It was best, wise men learned early, not to ask what women were thinking about at certain times.

"You've got the wrong idea about me. I can assure you of that."

This man's anger came from the confusion associated with being intimate with intensely passionate women. They said they were his, but they lied. They were everyone's. That was what made the fellow angry.

"I don't do that kind of thing."

One time a woman bragged to a man how much she liked to do it on top and how many times she could come. After that he never let her be on top again, and she had to be still as death waiting until he finished. She never understood what she'd said wrong.

"This isn't me, okay? This isn't the kind of thing I like."

That woman stayed with him, because she loved him and he was her husband and they were married and whatever it was that made him angry must have been her fault. I'm sorry, she said.

"Let's just back off, all right? Move over there. Move away."

Once a woman says I'm sorry, she's lost. Most men would rather hear that than I love you. It was best for a woman not to say I'm sorry because the fellows wanted to hear it again and again.

"Please?"

Some women, starting in the early 1970s, had begun to cause themselves problems from the intensity of their passion. Recently, the older women had tried to tell the younger women and the girls about the problems, but they wouldn't listen.

"You're really making this a bad scene," Mary said.

Remember the term *nympho?* It was popular in the fifties and early sixties. It's not used anymore. It's gone from the language.

"I'm going to scream really loud in a minute if you don't move out of my way."

The idea of the nymphomaniac actually worked for a long time and women did their best not to become one. It was a mean trick, though, because it referred to the few women who understood and enjoyed passion the way men did.

"GET AWAY!"

These women scared the hell out of men. Now so many women were like that the word and the idea of nymphomania were gone from the language.

"YOU CRAZY FOOL!"

Women used to lose their minds trying so hard not to be what they were or weren't. They drank a lot. They quietly suffered. They occasionally got committed to hospitals or killed themselves. It was like being at war, like their husbands had been, overseas, only they were fighting themselves.

"All right. Okay. Let's all just calm down. Let's take it easy. I think maybe we better call it a night. I don't feel well, actually. Something's made me sick," Mary said.

"How old is he?" Vincent asked.

He and his wife were watching Louise showing Walter the plantings, the garage her father had built, and other places of particular memory.

"Well, I don't know," Dorothy said.

"Wasn't the last one she dated older than her, too?"

"We don't talk about him."

"Wasn't he?"

"Don't bring it up."

"Don't do this. Don't do that," he said. "What the hell can I do?"

"And don't cuss."

The couple came inside. Louise was holding Walter's hand. He had to pry it loose to shake Vincent's. Dorothy hugged him and told him how much she'd heard about him.

"Do you follow the Braves?" Vincent asked.

For a long second Walter scrolled through sports memory to be clear what Vincent was talking about. He hadn't, actually, followed any baseball in years.

"I haven't been keeping up lately. How're they doing?"

Louise and her mother went to the kitchen, while Walter and Vincent settled down in the den.

"He's very nice," Dorothy said.

"Do you really think so?"

"I do."

"I hope Daddy doesn't run him off."

"He won't."

"I've been so worried about this meeting. Walter's parents are so dignified."

"I've heard of them. Someone, I don't remember who, used to go to Doctor Perkins, and someone else, Greta, I think, did too."

"He's such a quiet and sweet old man."

"Everything's going to be fine."

"You didn't tell Daddy anything?"

"Absolutely not. Who else knows?"

"Nancy. We haven't even told Walter's parents yet."

"I'm glad you brought him over. We watched you in the yard. He does seem very much in love with you."

"Oh, he is. He really is. I can't believe it. It's like I think he's going to come to his senses pretty soon and dump me, but so far, it's all just heaven."

"He'd be a fool to dump you, darling," her mother said. "You're going to be a wonderful wife. A wonderful mother. You'll do it all so much better than I did."

"I want to be wonderful."

Once at the table, Vincent began to do some serious eating, while everyone else ate a little, talked a little, and then ate some more. He had finished an inch-thick center-cut pork chop and all his mashed potatoes about the time that everyone else had only begun.

"Daddy? You were hungry."

"Huh?" he asked, looking up surprised, as if he'd forgotten anyone was there but him.

"How's work?"

"I can't talk," he said, chewing and then swallowing.

"Your mother said to be careful what I talked about, so I'm not going to talk about anything."

"Oh, Vincent, I said no such thing."

"The hell you didn't. Heck. I'm just going to eat," he said. "I'm about half-starved, late as it is."

"My parents always eat at six," Louise told Walter. "It's like a tradition."

"Or a law," her mother said, and the women laughed while Walter looked at Vincent to see his reaction.

"I ain't talking," he said, and filled his plate again.

"You know, strangely," Walter said, "we almost never talked at our meals, at home, I mean, when I was growing up. You could hear the ice melting in the glasses, it was so quiet."

"That sounds nice," Dorothy said. "So civilized."

"But it wasn't," Walter said. "It was like, even if you wanted to say something, you didn't feel like you should."

"Oh."

"Vincent, you can say anything you want. I think we ought to let her rip," Walter said.

At that, Vincent got up from the table, with his face red and beginning to sweat, and said excuse me and left the room.

"Did I say something wrong?" Walter asked.

"No. He just ate too much, too fast, as usual."

Much later, Vincent returned to the table and kept eating and they finished dessert, and then Louise and Walter cleared the dishes while Vincent disappeared once more, and then, while the women were washing and drying and talking in the kitchen, he pulled Walter over to the side.

"I got it bad," he whispered. "Really bad."

"What is it?"

"I got the damn diarrhea so bad you just better hope you never get in the shape I'm in."

"I'm sorry to hear that."

"I'm telling you," he said secretively, looking toward the kitchen to be sure the women didn't know what he was telling Walter, "I didn't think I was ever going to get out of that damn bathroom. I'm hurting bad now. I can't even sit down. Let me just tell you something, buddy. Just pray you don't ever get in the condition I'm in. The stuff," he said and then spoke even more softly, "was just going everywhere. Blood, too," he whispered, and then nodded at Walter as if he'd finally gotten to tell the truth, as if he'd finally gotten to be close to Walter in a way that meant something to him, as if they were finally open with each other, and connected, as if Walter was now privileged to know something he only told his closest friends.

Intimately bonded then, man to man, Vincent patted Walter on the shoulder and took him into the den, where he turned on the television, and together, sharing something further, they watched Vanna flip letters.

11

THE PHENOMENON of being swollen, of being engorged was delightful at times, especially at the release. Women caused the men to become engorged, and men, in turn, spilled over and got the women engorged. Women gave birth and everyone felt better for a while.

"I like that," Manny said. "Do it some more."

Shirley, who lived beside Walter's round house, had been brought up not to talk with her mouth full, so she said nothing about wishing she could go to sleep.

"Keep going," he said.

It was twelve-thirty at night and they had been in bed since eleven. There was a small skylight above the bed.

"Good," he said.

A person might think that, lying in bed at night, she could see, through the skylight, the stars and the moon and maybe, by chance, a meteor or a comet. She can't if the lights are on in the room, and Manny liked them on when he was with Shirley.

"Use your tongue more."

With the lamps on, the skylight was little more than a black square on the ceiling, like a hole in the roof, like a mistake, like an opening through which someone could enter and do you harm.

"Now you doing it, baby."

Southern women had often been taught to look down in modesty, especially in situations concerning men. Lately, a few of them had tried looking up, but that was risky. It exposed the throat and bared the neck and lifted the breasts like an offering.

"You learn good," he said.

Over the windows sheets and blankets were tacked with nails. Leaning against the wall was the curtain rod that Manny was going to hang when he had time. It was what Manny had hit Shirley with that once she deserved it.

"Slow down a little, gal."

Nothing else was in the room except their clothes on the floor and a television.

"Now you got it," he said. "Just like that."

The television was on the carpet. It was going to be nice when Manny let her have some money to buy a table for it.

"Don't stop," he said.

They'd had pizza for supper. She'd been burping up the taste of it all night long. Part of her tongue was numb where the cheese had burned it. It took pizza a long time to cool off, and she'd been hungry.

"All right. Go."

Once, when she'd been in Mexico with a boyfriend, she'd seen two children eat pieces of the cardboard from a box that pizza had come in. She saw this out the window of the car in which she was riding. It made her sad.

"Turn over," he said.

A RESPIRATORY THERAPIST helped people breathe. It was a relatively new profession.

In the past when people failed to breathe, they died. A person could live without food for a few weeks or without water for a few days, but without air he would suffer brain damage in a few minutes and die after nine or ten.

Some people thought they couldn't breathe when they actually could. This had to do with the periodic suffocation people felt at certain times in their lives. Of course, women felt it worst.

Louise could breathe well. She was, at this time in her life, clear of mind, of heart, and in her lungs.

For other people, however, it was her job to determine the capacity of their pulmonary systems. She analyzed the oxygen and carbon dioxide concentration, and checked on the acidity of the blood.

One of the saddest assignments for her was the premature infants whose lungs were not well developed. Seeing someone fighting for breath was not pleasant. Seeing a child fighting for breath was even worse. The Hollywood version of life simply slipping away couldn't have been more wrong. Force your hand over your mouth and nose and mash it without relenting. Do not let go. Try to die. You can't. You won't.

"We're going to his parents' house tonight," she told Nancy.

"How will that be? Fun?"

"Different. So, so different. My father, I swear, if I didn't love him, I'd do something. I don't know what. He embarrasses me so much."

"Did he say too much?"

"Too much? About what?"

"Anything. Anything you didn't want him to say."

"I guess. I mean yes."

"I hope he didn't. And I hope you haven't done that stupid confessional thing we all do where we tell our entire past to the man we're currently in love with. To the man who's got us in bed. Don't do that."

"In bed?"

"Oh, yeah. I forgot. Well, don't do it."

"I won't."

"Even if he asks. You'll pay for it if you do. I did. I told Mike everything, and now he throws it back at me whenever he wants."

"Yeah. I figured that one out. I know not to do that."

The air in the hospital itself was no better and likely much worse than the air outside and in other buildings. The air in the bottles hooked to the tubes that went into the noses or down the throats of the patients, though, was pure. Not pure oxygen, but a pure mixture of what it was the person needed.

That purity itself was not a monolithic matter meant more things could qualify as being pure than might have been thought.

"By the way," Nancy said, "did you find out his sister's name?"

Men often confused the idea of purity in thinking about

women. Purity, they thought, was an absolute, and embodied the elements of being chaste, guiltless, modest, and in general untainted by anything that hadn't come from them.

"Yeah. I knew it all the time. I just forgot. It's Mary."

CHAPTER 13

Louise and Walter were next scheduled to visit his parents to tell them about their engagement. She arrived at his house early and found him looking out the side window at his neighbor's backyard.

"Who's that?"

"Shirley's boyfriend. She's got a right to be there, but we didn't build the house for her and certainly not for him."

"What's wrong with him?"

"He worries me."

"How? He looks okay. More or less."

"A man with that kind of look on his face and spinning nunchucks? There's something about that whole scene that worries me. I don't believe that man would hesitate to use those on someone. Shirley, for instance."

"Why do you say that?" she asked, looking at the man's face to try to see what Walter saw.

"I've seen men like him before. They don't do right by women. That makes me mad. A man has an obligation to do right by women," Walter said. "Anyway, let's get going."

Louise enjoyed driving Walter in her car. Every boy she had ever dated insisted on driving. She could not recall one time when she'd actually driven one of her boyfriends anywhere. Walter seemed to enjoy it. He kept patting her on her leg and giving her affectionate punches on her arm whenever she drove, as if it amused and pleased him.

"I'm nervous," Louise said.

"There's no need to be. They adore you. They adored you the first time they met you. They already love you more than they love me."

"Of course they don't."

"Oh yeah? But it's all right if you don't believe it. In fact, it's sweet that you don't."

"You know parents love their children more than anything."

"Yes, they do. You're right," he said.

Mary Pristine was late. The family waited in the living room. Unlike Louise's house, where the television sets were on all day long regardless of whether anyone was actually watching them, this house was as quiet as a library.

"Well, Annie, shall we wait a bit longer?" Dr. Perkins asked his wife. "Did you call her again?"

"We should wait. I know she's on her way."

"Always late," her husband said.

"I'm here. I'm here," Mary called, coming down the hall. "You can quit talking about me now."

She dramatically scanned all the faces and then paused when she saw Louise.

"There she is. By golly, there she is. There's the woman who did what no other could do, and there were plenty who tried, dear one, plenty," she said and grabbed Louise's face in her hands and kissed her cheeks and then her lips. "She got him to say yes."

"He asked me," Louise said.

"I know, darling. We make them think that, don't we?"

"I did," Walter said.

Louise had been so curious about Mary and had anticipated meeting her for so long that it was as if she were meeting a celebrity or a legend. Walter had, little by little, told her about his sister and her adventurous and unsettled life.

"I'm so glad to meet you," Louise said, still unable to stand because Mary held her in her chair while she looked deeply into her face.

"That's enough, Mary," her mother said. "Leave the poor girl alone."

"But she's my sister. Soon to be."

"You're making her self-conscious."

"I am not, am I?"

"No, not really," Louise said and looked down and blushed.

"Oh my Lord, brother. She's shy. Oh, I love it. A shy woman. I didn't think they made them anymore. Leave it to you to find one."

"Come, Mary," her father said, taking her by the arm. "We've been holding supper."

"You're sitting beside me," she said to Louise. "Too bad, Walter. I got her for now. She'll never be the same again," she added and laughed at the worried look on her brother's face.

Walter hated his sister's manner and the way she lived, and he couldn't hide it. She had caused him so much concern and trouble all his life that he almost despised her for the mess she made of things. At the same time, he couldn't stop caring about her or helping her when she was down, listening to her tales of heartbreak and mistakes, sitting with her while she cried for hours or watching her fly high as a kite, deluding herself and becoming manic over whatever it was at the time.

It had distressed him to observe her life and seemed to have made him, early on, sympathetic to women, to all women, and had moved him to consider what it was in women that made their lives much more likely to be tragic than a man's. Tragedy and drama were a part of the lives of most of the women he'd known.

Louise went along with Mary like a puppy on a leash, like a kitten folded into someone's arms, caught up in another aspect of behavior he had noticed in women—the thrill they had of being desired, in any way.

"Don't believe anything she tells you about me," he said, "and not much else, either."

"You stay out of it, preacher man," Mary said, putting her arm around Louise. "Even though he talks and acts like one, I'm here to tell you, he ain't. Not at all."

"Settle down, Mary," her father said.

"I will, Daddy. I'll be so good, you'll think I've finally got religion."

After supper, Walter offered to help with the dishes.

"It's only before marriage they offer," Mary said, dismissing him so she and Louise could be alone.

"You know, I've never seen my dad do them. Never."

"See? I do know men. That's one thing I do know. But listen, Walter's different. He will be better than most. But you got to train all of them. *They won't learn by theirsayulves,*" she sang, trying to get a country music sound to it.

Walter and his parents were on the glassed-in sunporch. It was cool out there, as the central air conditioning had been ducted to that room, as well.

"I wish I could hear what they're talking about," he said.

Back in the kitchen, Mary was still running on about men and her family.

"You like how quiet it is here? Is that what you said?

Let me tell you something. It's the quiet that'll kill you. Ever been with a man who won't talk? Death. Absolute death. I'd rather be alone the rest of my life than with a man who won't talk."

"If you knew what my parents were like, you'd appreciate this."

"You know what we all need? A man raised by wolves, you know, and you find him and teach him everything."

"You're crazy."

"No, I'm right. But don't listen to me. Just because I don't like something doesn't mean you'd feel the same."

"Tell me anything you want. Go on. I want to know everything."

Mary looked at Louise's face. Her face was young and bright and full of hope. She didn't want to say any more. She didn't want to spoil everything.

"I'm sorry. Really, I am. I've had a terrible week and I didn't want to come here. Walter's right. Don't listen to me. And my parents are good people, and this was a good life we all had, all of us here when I was a child, and you're such a lucky woman to have found Walter because he is the nicest guy you'd ever be lucky enough to marry. He is. There's not a mean bone in his body. Not intentionally mean, anyway. He wants to be better than anyone else. He tries so hard. He does want to be so good. That's why I call him preacher man."

"I understand. I still want you to tell me everything, though."

"Let's finish up and go in with them. You're just what they've always wanted. I never was," Mary said and then stopped herself and chuckled and put her head on Louise's shoulder. "There I go again, feeling sorry for myself."

"I've got nothing on you," Louise said. "I'm as plain as a glass of milk."

"Forget that. I wish I'd been here when you told them. I bet they didn't suspect it. They'll be so happy now. They will. Good for you. Of course, now it'll be my turn again. I did it once, but that was so long ago. At least they gave up on the grandchildren thing from me. Now it's going to be on you. You're going to have to produce and fast before they get too old to enjoy them."

Back in the sunroom, the blinds had been closed. The setting sun was a deep and distant red glow through the slats. Bright, freshly painted white wooden porch furniture with flowered cushions invited both Walter and Mary to recall a childhood of many rainy days on this porch.

"This was my favorite room," Mary whispered to Louise as they approached. "The chairs and all are the same. Nothing's changed. That's nice. I think that's probably really a nice thing, that nothing's changed."

Dr. Perkins was smoking a pipe and blowing the smoke toward a tabletop air cleaner. His wife was working a crossword puzzle and talking to Walter, who pulled Louise onto his lap and kissed her before she settled down on the brick-red tile at his feet.

"Look at them," Mary said. "Isn't it perfect? Isn't it, Mom? And she's not even pregnant, so don't get to worrying about that. This is the real thing."

"Mary, I would never have thought such a thing in the first place."

"It's the first thing you two thought when I told you about me and Mister Wonderful, H. B. Calhoun. The very first thing."

Walter looked happier than anyone had ever seen him. He was in the midst of one of the highest points of any good man's life, the sweet heights of completing the act of desire, of giving a woman something she'd been wanting, of giving her something that she'd decided only he could give her. It was heroic, and everyone seemed to be made better by it. Being heroic suited Walter.

A charmed state of abandon seemed to be a part of this heroism. There was nothing so sweet on this earth as a happy woman who had given herself to a man, who had then, in return, given himself to her.

Women created a drama of their lives; they created parts for themselves to play and invited other people into the drama with them. Often, and inexplicably, the parts they created for themselves were difficult to perform, but they continued trying. Those parts were their lives.

Mary saw the drama of Walter and Louise and it touched her. It delighted her. It moved her. It also made her sad, considering her own dramatic failures.

"You two are going to be great. But you know what," she told them, unable to hide the tears in her eyes. "Stay away from me. Right, Mom? Right, Dad? I'm no good at all for the likes of you. I'm really not."

THE OTHER board members showed up soon after Walter and his friend John arrived at the Homes for Humanity office. John had requested they meet before the rest got there.

"So you're not going to stand by me?" Walter asked him at the last moment before the meeting began.

"I'll see."

This meeting had been called outside the ordinary schedule. It was a meeting Walter had been warned might be necessary.

"You know why we're here," the chairman said.

"I can guess," Walter told him. "But I still don't agree with you."

"We want you to understand where we're coming from. That's why we're all here again. We want you to understand, not only because we pay your salary but because we're right."

"Actually, you're not."

"You're a good administrator, Walter, and you're honest and efficient and pretty easy to get along with, most of the time. You work hard. You work longer hours than we pay you for, and though I understand you don't really need the money, we appreciate it. You certainly do your job."

"I try to."

"The point is, Walter, the black population of this city is twenty-seven percent of the total population. We have about six percent Hispanic, and then various minor percentages of other folks."

"It's about two percent Oriental now," someone said.

"But the loans arranged for, and the houses built for our clients are eighty-eight percent black-directed."

"That's what you said before, and like I said, they need it more."

"No, they don't. They did once, but they don't now. Need is need, and poor or disadvantaged whites need it the same."

"Not the way it looks to me."

"You're twenty or thirty years behind. Your thinking was right and we were wrong back then, but you're stuck there and now you're wrong."

"It seems to me the need is still there. It's the right thing to do to help these folks who need it so. It simply is."

"This is the last meeting we're going to have about this," the chairman said. "You know, I had some friends of some friends send people they knew about to you, and I know for a fact these folks were as poor as church mice and were as good a Christian family as you could find and you denied their application before we even got a chance to review it."

"Who was that?" Walter asked.

"You made a mistake there."

"I doubt I did."

After the meeting Walter and John walked to their cars together.

"You didn't speak up for me."

"There was nothing I could say. I warned you it was

coming. You've got to sign some white folks. I told you that last time."

"And I said I'd sign some when they needed it."

"Loosen up, bud," John said. "I'm telling you that for your own good. Just loosen up a little."

Walter had told Louise he'd be late. As she waited for him, she watched Manny and Shirley in their yard. He was using a string trimmer and now and again would aim it at Shirley.

"Stop it, Manny," she kept saying.

"I'm going to cut you, girl."

"Stop."

"I'm going to cut that pretty little leg."

When Walter returned home, she told him about Manny's actions.

"You know, I think they love each other. The way they played in the yard and the way he teased her and she flirted back with him, I'm sure he's okay."

"You're sure, are you, darling?"

"Absolutely. I can tell when people love each other."

Walter was so glad to be home from the meeting and to be with Louise. He thought, though, that she looked strangely tired and exhilarated and flushed, all at the same time.

"So, what about the big meeting?"

"Later. Tell me about your day first."

"I don't think I could until we eat. I'm starved."

Walter studied her as they ate. This is a woman, he thought, who would almost rather die than disappoint anyone, me or anyone else. This is a woman I could love forever.

"Shall we go in the other room?" he asked when they'd

finished. "You can tell me about your day and then I'll tell you about mine."

"I had an amazing day. A sad day but an amazing one. It was one of the all-time craziest," she said.

"Sad? How?"

"Well, you know how I've told you that when I get put on neonatal duty it gets to me worst, and the second worst days are when I get the cystic patients, who become my friends because they're close to my age, but then you know they're going to die, a lot of them, which makes it worse to become friends with them, of course. But today, I had to take three brain-dead children off their ventilators."

"Louise," he said, "why didn't you tell me earlier? You've been keeping this in? Why didn't you tell me?"

"It doesn't get to me usually. I can do anything, I really can. I sometimes think I can survive anything but then out of the blue, something like today gets to me. I'm sorry. Maybe I should have said something earlier. I was trying to be good company for you, especially because you seem worried about something yourself."

"Forget me," he said.

"It's just that you don't often have to deal with three in one day. Especially ones you've been working with for a while. One of them was a fifteen-year-old girl who had been complaining of headaches, really bad ones, for a long time, and her mom thought she was faking and wouldn't do anything for her, and then one day she found the girl holding her head and screaming in pain in the bathroom where she'd gone to try to get through it without bothering anybody.

"Then they brought her to ER, and by the time she got there, she was unconscious and unresponsive, and they did a scan and an MRI on her and it showed two aneurysms, and this was a couple of days ago that we got her, and I kept her on the ventilator all that time, and you could just tell from looking at her what a really sweet girl she was and her family was just horrible, I mean just horrible, like we had to work at it to get them to come see her, but finally today the family and the doctors decided to take her off the life support, and so I had to do it.

"They have all her organs and skin and eyes to be used, though, so something good came out of it. But I liked her. I just didn't want to see her go. So, anyway, that was number one.

"Then, number two was this four-year-old boy who'd been hit by a car while chasing a ball thrown by his father. I mean to tell you, this father was so hysterical, we had to sedate him. He was blaming himself bad. It was his fault because he said he made a bad throw and the boy had to chase it. The boy was adorable. He was wearing these little tennis shoes." Louise paused, almost bursting into tears as she thought about them, but then waved Walter away as he started to hold her and said, "I'm all right. It's just that there he was in these sweet little, tiny little tennis shoes, and they were so cute, it just got to me bad. But we worked furiously on him for hours. After a few hours, he was declared brain-dead, and I had to take him off the ventilator and he died. So that was number two. And under the sheet, he still had on those tennis shoes. I can't stand that. I'm going to see those little shoes forever.

"So that was number two. And then we got in this eight-year-old girl who'd been kicked in the head by a horse. I got sent back down to the pediatric ICU for her, and she was brain-dead already, but we tried, and then I had to take her off, and that was number three. It's terrible to see parents cry. It's just so sad. Usually we don't let them see us cry, but I couldn't hold it today. I just couldn't," she said, and then she covered her face with one hand and wept.

Walter had never seen her cry before. He'd never even

seen her sad. Most women he knew cried on a regular basis. Most cried at almost anything, from sad movies to being frustrated because he'd either done or not done something right or wrong, but Louise was the first woman he'd been with who never cried and never seemed sad.

"Sugar," he said, "I'm so sorry. Tell me what I can do."

"Nothing. I'll be fine."

He wiped her cheeks clean of the tears and got her a tissue to blow. Her face was red and hot and soft, and she looked so tender, it broke his heart.

"You know what, sweetheart," he said. "You've got to quit that job. You can't do this to yourself."

"No," she said, "I won't do that. I love what I do. I'm sorry I got upset. Really, I love my job," she told him, still crying.

"And I love you," he said. "So much, I do."

He began to kiss her, and the more he kissed her and the more he looked at her sweet, sad, beautiful face, the more he loved her. It was as if a part of her life he'd never known about was now revealed, and it touched him so to see how tender all things were for this trusting, exuberant, brave woman.

A half hour later, with her face still wet and red from crying, they made love. It was, of course, the first time they had made love. It seemed like the right time, and they were happy about it, and when they finished, Louise both laughed and wept and Walter stared across the room and out the windows to the sky and to the stars in wonder at how he had found a woman so perfect for him.

CHAPTER 15

FINDING a good woman was the luck of certain men. Before Walter found Louise, Vincent had discovered her mother, and the two of them lived in the seemingly stable state of being married, that is, being together come what may. Couples like Vincent and Dorothy were tied together in a way most of their children would never be. At least it seemed that way to those very children.

At the moment, Dorothy and Vincent were tied together even more closely, as he had her up on the roof with him with a rope loosely but securely looped around her waist. The rope led upward toward the top of the roof. Dorothy was braced on the slope and fed the rope over the peak. Holding the rope as it fed away from her and pulled against her, she could awkwardly rappel along the roof.

On the other side, across the ridge and out of sight, her husband was tied to the other end of the rope. Dorothy's weight kept him from falling off the steep pitch, as his kept her from slipping downward.

"Please, Vincent, please hurry."

As he went lower on his side of the roof, she rose up along her side toward him, rising and falling with his movements awkwardly and fearfully, looking like a corpse that was somehow alive, like a horse thief might have looked having been dragged behind the posse and then hauled up over a branch to be hung in the air, for all the townspeople to see.

"Dar, give me more slack."

He jerked downward on the rope and she tumbled forward.

"Good. Good girl. I can just about reach it now," he said and slid himself down the far side, while Dorothy did all she could to keep from losing him and at the same time keep herself from being flung over the peak and down the other side.

I am going to die this time. He is going to kill me this time.

"I can't hold on much longer," she said.

"What? I can't hear you."

She was trying to talk softly so that no neighbor would look out a window and see her up there.

"Just hurry up."

She felt herself getting weaker. Her legs were trembling as if she were in the electric chair being killed by a low dose of current.

"Just a few more minutes, Dar. Hold on."

He had a hammer in one hand and a pocketful of nails. He had finally figured out a way to nail back down the loose metal roofing on the garage that had been flapping in the wind for some time. By hooking his wife to the other end of the rope, he could maneuver up and down and side to side as long as she followed, on the other end, on the other slope, pulling back against him as she did.

"I'm going to fall," she said.

She had not understood what it was he wanted her to do. She thought it had something to do with holding a rope while he went up on the roof, alone. Then it seemed to her it had to do with her getting on the ladder for just a minute and tying the rope to something. Then it was something about tying it to her waist, as well, to make it more secure. Then suddenly she was on the roof.

"Please God," she said, "please get me down."

"What?" he called back. "Are you all right?"

"I've got to get down," she said, louder this time.

"I am going down. Just a couple more feet. There's that last piece over there that's been flapping every time we have a storm from the west."

Each was out of sight of the other, and Vincent could not see that Dorothy had fallen over frontward and was now lying on the roof like a bag of sand. When she fell frontward, the rope went a couple of feet slacker than he'd wanted on his side.

"Damn, Dar. Pull back."

He moved further down his side, and the rope tightened up. From then on as he moved around at that level, Dorothy was dragged side to side and slid up and down like a dead weight, like a boxer's punching bag, only instead of tan canvas, it was purple and light green, the colors of her blouse and skirt.

"Vincent," she called out.

"Tighten up now," he said. "I'm coming up."

As he did, she slid downward. She looked behind her and saw the edge of the roof coming and struggled to her knees and then back to her feet.

"Just easy does it," he called just before his face appeared at the ridge. "That's a girl, easy does it."

She found the ladder and slowly climbed down. Her skirt was sideways and her blouse had lost three buttons.

"When you get on the ground, walk around to the other side and give me some tension on the rope so I can get down to the ladder," he said.

After he was on the ladder, she tried to untie the rope,

but the knot had tightened up and she couldn't do it. She walked toward him just as he loosened his knot, picked up his hammer, and started inside the garage.

"Thanks, Dar. You're a gem," he said and disappeared inside, leaving her standing in the side yard, tied to a rope for anyone to see, a woman pale of face and trembling of lip and leg, with a one-inch rope knotted around her and, from what anyone from the road could see, the other end tied somewhere around the back of the house, so she couldn't run away, maybe?

It would have been difficult to guess, driving or walking by and taking a glance, the what and the why and the story of that woman's life.

C H A P T E R 16

DOWN ON HERSELF even more, Mary was on her way to see Dr. Mullet, with whom she had finally gotten an appointment.

Dr. Sue Mullet had a large head. Her face was coarse and mannish, and though she wore expensive clothes, she was short, squat, and overweight and looked like a peasant from wartime newsreels. Her legs were too thin and toddled under her torso like sticks stuck in a baked potato. She looked top-heavy.

She had grown up poor on an unmodernized pig farm in Georgia, and though she had worked on her resentment of the rich and glamorous, she could not quite defeat it.

Had Mary known that Sue Mullet had always disliked her, had envied her good looks and her money and her easy way with people, she would never have booked herself in with this woman.

She was, though, an expert on sexual matters, and Mary assumed her problems were that, since it was men she thought about nearly all the time.

Dr. Mullet herself knew about new research on odd symptoms of distress in women of passionate and uninhibited activity. She knew the most common symptoms of either too much sex or too intense sex for women were migraine headaches, buzzing in the ears, blurred or distorted vision, swollen spleens, blackouts during the act, difficulty hearing on occasion, seeing food on a plate as something else, loss of taste sensations, and a weak feeling in the arms and thighs, with unusual emotional highs followed by unusual lows.

Some problems had been understood years earlier, such as the loss of taste sensation, which was linked to having had, over a short period of time, too much semen in the mouth.

While Dr. Mullet knew all of the latest theories and symptoms, she held that women, more often than men, had become stuck during the conception process in the fallopian tubes of their mothers, and the trouble these women had in either expressing themselves too little, or in going too far, related to having been stuck in the tube for so long.

The method Sue Mullet had devised to help these people was to have them fight, literally, their way out of a large replica fallopian tube in a room adjacent to her office. There were people all day long screaming and punching and kicking their way out of their mothers' fallopian tubes.

Toward the end of Mary's first visit, Dr. Mullet began to think she would benefit from this therapy.

"I'm so miserable," Mary said, "and talking doesn't do a bit of good. I've been here a half hour and told you everything I could fit in and remember to say about why in the hell I go out with men like Rob, and so, after all this, do I feel any better?

"No. And I want to feel better. You know what I want? I want to learn how not to think anymore. I'm sick of thinking. I'm sick of knowing that something's wrong with me or seeing that something's wrong with someone else or wondering what this person or that person's going to be like and then actually taking it on myself to find out, which usually ends up with me getting hurt. I'm sick of all of that. I want to just go out there and be. I want to be like I was when I was younger, before I knew any damn thing at all.

"I'm stuck," she said, and Dr. Mullet's ears perked up like a dog's hearing a whistle. "I just can't get past ... I don't even know what it is I can't get past. I can't get past being me."

"You can."

"I don't know. I want to be what I was long ago when I was just who I was without thinking about it and before all the hell I did to myself started. I see these young women and I think, darling, don't lose it. I want to tell them what might happen when they go wrong and for them not to go wrong and to be careful and all that, but so far, I haven't. I just look at them and feel sad and jealous."

"You can cry here. It's all right."

"I don't want to. I just want to change."

"We all do. And we can change. It's finding out how, and where to go with the change."

"Right."

"Usually, this confusion and frustration and sense of helplessness began long ago."

"Not for me. I was clear as a bell when I was a kid. Clear as a damn bell."

"You were clear when life was less complicated and when you didn't have to make choices. It's the choices that bring us down."

"Maybe so. Maybe you're right. My childhood was heaven. I was okay all the way up to my late teens."

"You think you were."

"I don't think I was. I was, plain and simple. I was."

"To others seeing you at that time, you might not have been."

"I was. Forget that part of it. I was fine. You can ask my brother, and he thinks I'm a lunatic now."

"Let me propose something to you. I think it might work, from what I hear you say, and I would advise you to take what I'm going to say seriously," Dr. Mullet added, sensing how most of what she'd already told this woman had been given back to her in denial. "Try to consider what I have to offer."

"All right."

She began then to tell Mary about the fallopian tube theory and how the treatment worked and what she had seen in her patients as they went through the schedule. She spoke slowly and quietly so Mary would have to listen intently. After a while, Mary looked down, into her lap, and put her face in her hands.

"It's all right. I know you're frightened. It's okay to be afraid. It's part of the trauma of being conceived so violently, in one sense."

Mary looked up then and, unable to contain herself any longer, burst out laughing.

"I'm sorry," she said, "but listen. I was doing all I could not to get hysterical over what you were saying, but I couldn't hold it in. I mean, really, are you telling me you're serious? I mean, it sounds like something from *Saturday Night Live*. I'm just too sorry, but I don't think I could do that."

"You need it. You need it badly. You are in denial of so much."

"I don't deny anything. I know I'm a mess."

"Your nervous laughter tells me how much fear there is in you."

"It isn't fear. Believe me."

"You must trust me if we're going to work together."

"Yeah, I know that. I do trust you. I guess. But don't put me in that tube. Please don't put me in that tube," she said, almost laughing again.

"There've been many people helped this way."

"Let's think of something else."

Sue Mullet then hated her as much as she did whenever she heard about Mary's escapades or saw her at a social function, saw her beautiful clothes and moneyed high-class manner so casually Scarlet O'Hara-ed all over the place.

"Do you want to become well?"

"Sure."

"Or do you want to spend the rest of your life a miserable, insecure, masochistic wreck?"

"Well, good Lord, it's not that bad, is it?"

"Isn't it?"

"Not all the time. I mean, not even most of the time. Sometimes, maybe. I guess."

"You should do what I say."

"I can't do that particular thing."

"You need it."

"There must be something else."

"This is better."

"Nope."

"Are you sure?"

"Fairly sure. I mean, yes, I am miserable, and, yes, I want your help. I do mean that."

"I can't help you unless you do what I say. You must do what I tell you, think the way I ask you to, and follow my directions. You must agree to that, and I sense you are not going to," she said, not wanting to work with her at all by now.

"I want you to help me. I do want help."

"Then you'll do what I tell you to do."

"I could try."

"I don't think you would," she said.

"I would, though."

"I don't think we could work well together. I don't believe this is going to be a successful therapeutic relationship."

"Well, who could I see then?"

"I don't know. I couldn't advise you on that. Our time is up, anyway. Good luck, Mary," she said and looked away, hoping she'd be gone when she looked back.

"Can't you think of someone?"

"No."

"Well, thanks a lot then. Damn."

"Our time is up."

"Well, screw you."

"See that door?" Dr. Mullet said, standing behind her desk.

"Yeah, I see that door."

"Use it."

"Use it?"

"GET OUT OF MY OFFICE!"

Mary looked at her then. Dr. Mullet's face had become red and raw and bloated. For a moment it looked as if a skinned head of a sow had been set on the little body teetering behind the desk. It freaked Mary out how fast the woman's anger had transformed her.

"I'm out. You bet I am."

It scared her, too. The whole thing scared her. The Miss Piggy Muppet-look of the woman, the hostility from her, the way nothing at all had gone right. She was shaking as she got in her old car. She drove slowly and felt worse than ever.

She wanted to talk to someone more than ever, as well. She was tired of mean people and tired of fighting with them, of falling out with them, of always choosing the wrong person, even the wrong therapist. She wanted, most of all, to see Louise and to talk to her more than anyone else on this earth she could think of.

Louise was at work when Mary called. She had just had a rare laugh as she watched her supervisor microwave a hot dog for six minutes. Microwaving funny things was one of her supervisor's hobbies, and the staff looked forward to these experiments. Microwaving medical equipment always brought about a vengeful, crazy level of laughter that, Louise thought, was out of proportion to how funny it actually was.

"Sure," Louise said, "we can meet, but not for lunch. I might not even get a lunch break today. I often don't."

There were other strange ways of dealing with the difficult job, and one of them—playing poker for the worst patients—had been Louise's idea. Although she knew this was mean and although her heart broke at times for the poor suffering souls, the poker and microwaved tubes brought relief from the fatigue of long hours and sad patients.

"I'd love to see your house. I'll be there after work."

Mary's house was one of those in-town estates that Louise had admired all her life. She thought it was a shame that Walter had built such a weird design, but maybe there would be a time when they would have something like this.

"I'm going to faint," Louise said. "It's just that beautiful."

"Don't look too close," Mary said. "It's run-down and dirty and shabby as a hobo's camp."

"I doubt that," she said, wide-eyed and smiling so

brightly that Mary thought she'd not seen in years such a happy person.

"Do you feel this good all the time, or is this just an act for your future in-laws?"

"I feel extra good today. Extra good."

"I'm glad somebody in this family feels good."

"I'm not in the family yet."

"You're in it. You're there, Louise. Walter wouldn't let you go if he had to die to keep you."

"You're sweet to say that."

"I'm not sweet. But it's true."

"You're like Walter. I tell him he's this or that, and he always denies it. You seem sweet to me."

"Sit down, Louise. I feel like talking. Do you want some wine?"

"I guess. Sure."

"You probably never drink, right?"

"Not often."

"I know. You don't even NEED to drink, right? You're so dad-gummed pure you don't even need it."

"I need it sometimes. You just haven't seen me at my worst."

While Mary was in the kitchen, Louise looked up the wide stairway at the old pictures on the wall, wondering if they were family ancestors, and at the furniture and the Oriental carpets, which, though it seemed odd to her, were on top of the wall-to-wall carpeting. Her mind moved forward in time to her and Walter and their children, all cavorting around a house like this, with her at the center of things, her children calling her, her husband needing this or that and she giving it, simply flying back and forth, being so good and so satisfying that the whole world around her was happy and content.

"I've already had two glasses," Mary said. "I've been sitting here feeling bluer than blood."

"Yeah, I see that blue color a lot," she said. "Faces and lips pale blue as summer sky."

"Well, I'm bluer than that, and I've been drinking too much, so years from now when you think about me, cut me some slack."

"You can tell me anything."

"Strange," Mary said. "I should be saying that to you. Wait here. Don't move. I got to go to the bathroom."

Women talked, and this was good. The words were different. The styles were different. That was because forty or fifty years ago women did not know what they know now. They thought if things were bad in their marriage, it was their fault. The doctors put the pitiful, suffering, depressed post–World War II housewives on Miltown or amphetamines, and the women quickly went daffier. They had to drink themselves into numbness. Some ran away, but most stayed and endured.

Not that much has changed.

Back then, women wore bizarre bras manufactured to come to points, which they wore under dresses or tops that had, in the bodice, material gathered into points, as well.

Nothing has changed except the technology. The poor confused women now have their breasts stuffed with silicone, giving them the deformed, swollen look of erect tissue, and then what? Bras that take those deformed, cartoonish breasts and push them up over the neckline and into your face.

"Our mothers had it so much easier," Mary said, flopping back down on the couch.

"They did?"

"Oh yeah. They just plugged in and went for it."

"I don't know about that," Louise said. "They suffered."

"You know, when I was your age, I was married to Mister Harris B. Calhoun, of the South Carolina Calhouns."

"Gosh."

"You're right, little girl," Mary said, now very much finished with an entire bottle of wine herself, while Louise was staring at only her second glass and unable to drink it. "I made the best marriage any sweet-assed, pure-as-driven-snow Southern belle could make. Mister Harris B. Calhoun."

"Did they really ask you if you were pregnant?"

"Hell yes they did. Daddy is a doctor, don't forget. He saw girls coming in his office pregnant and scared and crying and asking him what to do, hoping somehow he might do an abortion, which none of them, and I mean none of them back then, except the wino doctors, would do. But I wasn't, which was a miracle, except for the fact that my mother had explained the menstrual cycle to me, and I had it in the back of my head, way in the back, I might say, the whole time me and Mister Calhoun were doing what we did.

"Daddy, being a doctor, and a distinguished one at that, only gave me this advice and information when he talked to me about it. He said, Mary, watch yourself. Be careful. Just watch out for these boys. And that was all he said, I swear, except for the AMA booklets they gave me to read, that was it. Be careful. If it hadn't been for Mom, I would have been pregnant ten times before I was twenty. I'm sure of it.

"But I wasn't going to talk about that. I was going to talk to you the way someone should have talked to me. Because I made a mess of things, and I'm still doing it, and it seems everything I did wrong has stayed with me, and I don't think young women know that. Do they? Do you? I bet you don't. I bet you have never thought that every mistake you make will stay with you forever. It's like marrying a really bad man, and you have children with him, and then you divorce him, but the children are JUST LIKE HIM, and you've got them forever, and then they turn on you and treat you just like he did, and you can't ever get away, and that's what people don't realize."

The way Louise was looking at her, it dawned on Mary that she was out of control.

"Listen, I'm sorry. I went to a therapist today and this stuff started coming out of me and then she tried to talk me into doing some stupid therapy and I walked out and then I thought about you and how young you are and I wanted to tell you that I love you already and I know we're going to be great sisters, and that's really what I wanted to say, that I love you and am thinking about you."

"I love you, too, Mary. I love your whole family."

"I'm going to have another glass of wine. This'll be my last, though. I promise. You talk to me now. I've been talking too much. Tell me something."

"Like what? How much I love your brother?"

"No. Don't tell me that. We all love Walter. Tell me something else. Like, tell me a dream you've had. I like dreams."

"A dream?"

"Yes. Something from your childhood. A recurring dream-type thing. I'll tell you one I used to have later."

"Well," Louise said, "I know there was one. But I haven't thought about it in so long. But I know there was one I used to have all the time. What was it?"

"Mine are rolling around in my head, all the time."

"I remember now. The chicken dream."

"I love it."

"The chickens. Gosh. Those damn chickens used to

scare me so bad. I haven't had the dream in a long time, though. But the way I remember it is I used to wake up and in my room would be these huge chickens. I mean, huge, like as big as people. I would try not to open my eyes, but I would, and then they'd be there, and they'd make me get out of bed and squat on the floor and lay an egg.

"I wouldn't be able to do it, though, and they'd make me, and I couldn't leave the room until I did. I know it doesn't sound scary, but it was. The chickens would chase me into my parents' room and they'd be in there with me, and I'd be screaming, LOOK OUT, HERE THEY ARE! and all that. Those damn chickens used to come in the night a lot."

"Did you ever do anything on the floor?"

"Like what?"

"Like a BM, Louise. What do you think?"

"No."

"I would have. If those chickens had been making me squat like that, I would have."

Louise looked at her watch, but Mary didn't notice. She was in a hurry to get to Walter's house. They hadn't had much time to talk about the night before.

Vincent was in the living room. He had finished supper and was rereading the morning paper.

"I wish they still had afternoon papers. It gave a man something to read when he got home."

They'd had a big supper. Dorothy had made spinach casserole with breaded, spicy baked chicken and corn on the cob from their own garden, as well as a cherry pie, this time just for him.

"Them fools on the television news all talk the same talk, and all at the same time. You can turn from one network to the next, and all of them are talking the same story at the same time."

Dorothy had had a wonderful afternoon playing bridge with three of her friends. They'd been playing cards together and talking and baking sweets for each other for more than twenty years.

"Did you notice how all of them decided at one time that all them local militias were a bunch of nuts. They all get the same party line."

Dorothy had not been as hungry as she might usually have been because one of the women had made the most wonderful lemon and caramel tarts she'd ever had in her life. Her friend Betty Jane had made tiny pie shells and then filled one or the other with her own caramel or lemon filling.

"You know," Vincent said, looking over the top of his paper, "some of them bombings are done by the federal government. That's what some people say."

Dorothy was looking through a women's magazine. She was looking at an article about a house in Mississippi. The furniture inside was breathtaking, and the place settings on the dining-room table were just to die for. She had never in her life seen such a beautifully set table.

"You know David? He's in one of those groups. He runs around on the weekends shooting dummies set up in the woods."

Another one of the articles in the magazine was about a mother and daughter who'd started their own bakery and made pies and cakes for restaurants and weddings and banquets. Louise had always been a terrific cook and used to love to hang out in the kitchen when she was making supper or baking.

"Lord, that hurt," he said. He had just leaned over sideways in his chair and passed some gas.

She didn't think she could read the article now, but she was going to save it and, when Vincent went to work tomorrow, read it then.

"God almighty," he said. "That's a terrible one," he mused, sniffing the air and concentrating on the smell. "I wonder what in the hell that was." He sniffed some more and then said, "I believe that was that spinach. Damn if I don't. Either that or the stuff you sprinkled on the chicken."

MANNY was teaching himself the use of nun-chucks. It looked simple but it was not.

The nunchucks, two short truncheons the size and length of a person's forearms, but heavier and as dense as the ash wood they were made out of, were linked together end to end with a chain. By twirling one and holding the other, a person could create a great deal of force on impact when the one zinging in a circle suddenly struck.

The problem with learning the nunchucks was that you hit yourself hundreds of times before you got it right.

"I can't carry a gun, you know," Manny said.

He was prevented from doing that by the terms of his probation.

"They didn't say nothing about this stuff," he said, and whirled the sticks in the air like he'd seen on the martial-arts video he and Shirley had watched last night, before they put on the one about the woman who gets sent to hell and has to do everything the men down there want her to do.

"Can I get you something to drink?" Shirley asked. "It's so hot out here. I wish those trees would grow."

"I don't drink when I'm working out."

"Do you have a couple of dollars left? I could maybe

get us some hamburger and some buns, and we could have a cookout."

"Yeah. In a minute."

The nunchucks were brown with a dark stain finish. One of the ways you could disable someone with them was to wrap them around the person's neck and choke him, using the heavy sticks for leverage. You didn't have to choke him to death, but you could at least cut the circulation and make him black out, the way cops always did when they could get away with it.

"Hi," Shirley said, waving to Walter.

"I don't like him," Manny said. "Don't be so friendly."

"He's all right. He's the bossman for these houses."

"He was the bossman. Your sister owns it now. I don't see the need to be so friendly with him anymore."

"Okay, Manny."

"You can't keep your eyes off him, can you?"

"I don't care a thing about him," she said.

CHAPTER 19

MARY ALMOST FELL asleep on the couch while Louise was talking to Walter on the phone. The Xanax she had taken before she started drinking was feeling good. Usually, it didn't have much effect on her.

"Sit down," Mary said. "I know you have to go. A man is calling you. When he calls you, you got to go. It's the law. It's the law of a woman's life. And when no man calls for you, you don't exist. What is the sound of a woman with no man?"

"I don't believe that," Louise said.

"Crying. That's the sound. Your generation is worse than mine. You are man crazy like we never were."

"Oh, come on, Mary."

"But that's neither here nor there. The thing is, I want to give you some rules to live by. Get the paper over there, and that pen. Now, write down what I say to you. Just copy it down word for word.

"Number One. No young man, no male under the age of twenty, will be allowed to have sex with any woman unless he is married to her. This is because the young men don't deserve it, because they don't earn it, and it ruins them, forever, ruins them completely once they see what they can do to us.

"Number Two. Never date, marry, or even go out with any man over forty who drives a two-seater sports car. Never, you understand, Louise? Write it down. These men are bottle-sucking, narcissistic losers, and you won't get anywhere with them.

"Number Three—and I just learned this one late in life—never hang out with, date, and marry an academic man, especially a literature professor. These men are total losers and somehow imagine that they know more than anyone else about everything, including YOUR life. These men hold the world record for arrogance and coldness. They're the reason the feminist movement began. All the women who started it had been married to academic men. It's also going to take at least three porno films, handcuffs, and an enema to give them an erection."

"I'm not going to write this down," Louise said.

"You should."

"I'm marrying Walter. I won't need to think about this, and anyway, you know you can't generalize about men or anybody for that matter."

"You sure as hell can."

"Look, Mary, I've got to go. Walter's got supper ready. Don't be mad at me for leaving. I'm sorry. We'll get to-gether another time and you can finish the list then."

$\mathbf{A}$LTHOUGH MANNY had not read a book since he was in the eighth grade, which is as far as he got, he had seen many films and lots of television.

Because it must have been an easy thing to do, to make a film where a woman was endangered, or because it was what the men making the films most enjoyed, themselves, that is, stalking or terrifying or rendering helpless good-hearted, trusting women, most of the films that Manny had seen involved the servitude or degradation of one or more women. Because there was for Manny something thrilling about this, it seemed only natural and certainly understandable that he might want to act out one of these scenarios.

Since Manny was not a bad man, at least not as bad as some, there had to have been a reason for him to tie Shirley to the telephone pole in front of Walter's house, and to gag her, and to string her head tightly against the pole with a thin wire, just below her hairline, so that she had to look up and could not hang her head in shame.

Some men, worse off than Manny, would get a thrill out of something like this all on its own. Manny had a reason and wouldn't have done it otherwise.

"She called your name," Louise said as she and Walter watched the paramedics and the police take her down.

"I know."

"They might think you did it."

"I'm sure they know who did it. I'm sure they know him very well, from one thing or another."

Shirley slipped from the hands of her rescuers and when she did, she fell backward and took the one who tried to catch her with her.

"I'm sorry," Louise heard her say. It seemed she had said that. It seemed she had apologized for falling over.

"This is awful," Louise said. "Just awful."

"It is awful," Walter said.

"Should we tell them what we think? Is he even here? I mean, shouldn't we tell them it was probably Manny?"

"If it was."

"Oh."

"I hate this."

"Me, too," she said. "It's so odd. It's so weird to wake up to this, after that," she said and put her arm around him and nodded toward their bedroom. "What a strange thing, that we could go from that to this."

About the time that Shirley rode away in the ambulance, Dorothy awakened and noticed not blue lights or sirens or any other signals of emergency but, instead, the muted glow of the hall light coming from under her door. She listened for sounds and heard nothing. Vincent, whose room was next to hers, slept like a dead man each night, so it would have been unusual for him to be awake. Maybe he was sick.

She opened the door and was startled to meet him face to face directly in front of the door, as if he'd been about to knock.

"What is it, honey?" she asked, actually hearing the

word *honey* come out of her mouth from some time or some feeling long ago.

"I was trying to hear if you were awake. I don't know why you would have been."

"You could have come in."

"I didn't want to bother you."

"What is it?"

"I was thinking about Louise."

"What about her?"

"She's going to marry that man. It sort of hit me, is all. I don't know that I like him."

"You don't? I think he's wonderful."

"He's too old for her."

"Vincent, no father ever wanted his daughter to marry anyone."

"I guess that's so, but there's something."

"Sit down, honey," she said and patted the bed. He stood by the edge while she got back under the covers.

"You think she's going to be happy with him?"

"Very happy. She's already happier than she's ever been, and I'm sure he'll be good to her. I am sure of it."

"Is she going to quit her job?"

"I don't know."

"Is she going to have children right away?"

"Ask her."

"I can't do that."

"You can."

"You ask her for me," he said.

"What, now?"

"Hell no, not now, Dar."

He had run out of anything to say, and the minute or so when no words filled the empty space between him and his wife was a long minute for him.

"I know I ain't no good as a father. You raised her. I

mean, except . . . you know. I never did know what to do."

"You did fine."

"Where's she going to live?"

"With her husband. Like I did."

"Yeah, but this was your momma's land we built on. I don't think it's going to be the same."

"You look so worried," she said. "Come lie down here awhile. Take it easy."

"I can't sleep. I got the upset stomach. I feel so nervous."

"Here," she said and patted the bed again. "Settle down here until you feel better."

"I'm all tensed up. I shouldn't have drunk that Pepsi before I went to bed."

"Here," she said. "Come here. It'll be nice. It'll be cozy. You'll feel so much better."

"I got to go," he said and rushed toward the door.

"Coward," she whispered.

"Huh?"

"Go to bed," she said.

When Shirley returned home from the emergency room the next morning, Walter and Louise went to see her. A row of sutures held a horizontal slit together in her forehead at the hairline where the wire had cut into her scalp. It looked like a deformed second mouth, grinning with narrow black teeth clenched together.

"It's not so bad," Walter said.

"It doesn't look that bad at all," Louise said, meaning it, since she had seen worse.

"I look awful," Shirley said. "And don't ask me what you're going to ask me. Just don't."

"If he did it, then you've got to press charges."

"I said don't ask me about it. I don't want to talk about it."

"I'll do it for you, if you're afraid. And you can move in with us," Walter said, "or we'll find you a safe place."

"He hit her, too," Louise said, looking at her face.

"He didn't do it."

"Who did?"

"Nobody. Me. I don't know."

"What did you tell the police?"

"That I didn't remember what happened. That I did it to myself."

"You know they don't believe you."

"That's what they wrote down."

"You've got to let us help you. Where is he?"

"I guess he's at work. Why wouldn't he be?"

"Don't do that, Shirley. Don't play with us. We're your friends," Louise said.

"Aren't you a nurse? Haven't I seen you in your uniform?"

"Yes."

"I'd like to be a nurse. I'm not smart enough, though."

"Listen, Shirley," Walter said. "It's obvious to anyone that Manny did this to you. Just tell us, in confidence, if you want to, if that's the only way you'll tell us, why and what happened. If you want it that we won't tell anyone, that we won't tell the police, then that's the way it'll be."

"You swear?"

"I swear."

"You aren't going to have him arrested?" Louise asked.

"He didn't mean it. He loves me. He already called me this morning, and he was crying he was so upset."

"Why did he do it?"

"Because of something I did. I did something wrong."

"What'd you do wrong?" Louise asked. She'd had this

conversation with countless women in the hospital. Some of them wanted to kill whoever had hurt them, and some only wanted to get back in his arms and die some more.

"You wouldn't understand."

"I would. I'm a woman. You can tell me."

"He wouldn't."

"Walter, go home for a while and let us talk."

He left. He noticed there was no evidence of a fight in the house itself.

"You know how jealous men can be?" Shirley asked.

"I sure do. Before I met Walter, darn near every boy I dated was a raving fool that way."

"Well, don't tell Walter this, but it was about him."

"Uh oh," Louise said, thinking that she was about to hear something from the past she didn't want to know.

"I spoke to Walter yesterday, and Manny didn't like it, and then I made it worse by saying what a really nice guy he is, and I knew better because Manny just hates it when I talk about other men, so he got mad about it in the middle of the night after he had sex with me and accused me of thinking about Walter while we were doing it, which I wasn't, and so he stuck me out there facing his house so I could think about him some more, he said. Please don't tell anybody. Really, he's so sorry now, I could make him crawl across nails and he'd do it."

21

Two weeks later, Manny was back home. It seemed to Walter that he and Shirley were back to whatever their idea of normal was.

Then, knowing it might happen but still caught by surprise, Walter was asked to resign as head of the housing program.

Two weeks after that, he and Louise were married by a retired Methodist minister who was a longtime friend of Dorothy's, as well as her ex-pastor. Mary Pristine cried and drank too much.

Having the money to go anywhere, Walter decided to take Louise to a house in the Blue Ridge Mountains in Allegheny County.

The house was owned by a friend of his family's, and he had spent many summers there as a child. The house was a home to him unlike his own childhood home. There had always been graciousness and kindness and warmth in the house. He told Louise about his summers there so that she would love it the way he had.

From the deck off the back of the house, they could see as far as the eye could see. At times, they could see what seemed like fifty miles of rolling valleys and peaks of mountains as unspoiled and tree-covered and virginal as they must have been hundreds of years ago.

In the valleys, in clearings, people came out of the little houses and moved around like figures in a miniature drama, and cars left the clearings and disappeared into the trees.

Clouds came and went, and thunderstorms blew up, and they watched them boiling toward them, leaving the air heavy and charged by lightning.

In the night, animals called out as possums walked on the roof, and Louise was too happy to understand how it ever could have been that she had not known this bliss. Walter was thrilled at her happiness and delighted to be able to give it to her.

He loved her, but only her, the way she loved all of life itself. This charmed him but also worried him, and it would be, he thought, that he would have to protect her from this love of life itself.

A week later they returned to Chapel Hill. It was now clear to Walter that a house at some distance from the town, in which life was lived at a different pace with a vision and a focus unique to that house and to the family within, would be right for himself and Louise.

It was also clear to Walter that there was no reason for him to support this community in the way he'd once thought important, that is, to champion the cause of people's need for housing, and to live among those people. There could be a better way and a cleaner way and a purer way, it seemed, for him.

With these two understandings in mind, he sought advice and quickly bought the loveliest old farmhouse he could find that was close enough to town for Louise's commute and that was in relatively good structural condition.

The house was on sixty-eight acres of land. He rented his carnival of a house in town and, along with it, his past, and he and Louise moved away.

ATOMIC WOMAN

In THE FALL, about six weeks after Louise and Walter moved from town, a man appeared on the streets. No one knew who this man was.

He didn't know who he was, either. This might not seem unusual in the age where psychology had so thoroughly replaced religion that instead of being told who you were within the limits of theological determination, you were always questioning who you were, and no one knew anything. I don't know who I am was a common phrase spoken during this time. I don't know what I am supposed to do or how I am supposed to be.

Women had it worse because they were supposed to be even more of whatever it was they were, even if they did not know what that was.

This man not only didn't know who he was, he didn't even know his name.

He didn't know what town he was in or what his parents had done or not done to make him be where he didn't know he was. He was just plain old-fashioned lost and down and out.

This man was actually better off than the average hobo or tramp or homeless soul, because after the police picked him up and had him evaluated, it was determined that he had amnesia. This man, who was in his late thirties or early forties, couldn't feel too bad about himself because he didn't know if he'd ever done anything to feel bad about. He was a lucky fellow.

He was amoral in that he didn't know right from wrong, but not analgesic, because he could feel pain. With the right help, he would also be able to understand good and evil in the world, if the authorities decided that was the proper thing to teach him.

Because he was so attractive and bright and cheery, as well as sad and tragic and vulnerable, all in a curiously quaint way, the women who read about him in the paper and saw him on the news went bananas. The Department of Social Services had not only a long list of their own workers who wanted to take him in but also a thousand calls from women all over the country who wanted to marry him.

A radio station ran a contest to name him, promising the winner five hundred dollars and the possibility of lunch with the man, if it could be arranged.

The staff at the station chose the entry that named him Zephyry because, they said, it sounded like a real name, as in Jeffrey, but wasn't, and because it could mean a gentle breeze, a zephyr, which, the entrant said, was the way the man made her feel, like a cool breeze had come into her life.

"I love it," Louise said to Nancy as they took a quick break and scanned the paper on their way to see some patients. "I just think it's the neatest thing."

"I don't know."

"But it is. I'd love to meet him."

"You don't actually imagine he's sane, do you? You don't think he's happy being out of it, do you?"

"Why not?"

"I don't think he could be. I think amnesia victims are miserable and lost and scared half to death."

"He doesn't seem to be."

Three patients had come in together. Number one was a woman, number two was her boyfriend, and number three was a policeman.

Pieced together later from all that Louise and Nancy could learn, it turned out that number one had been having sex with number two, her boyfriend. She then left him in bed and went out the door, nude, directly into the path of a car.

Number one, on admission, was still having the by now recognizably spontaneous orgasms with lulls of unconsciousness in between and asystolic vascular activity and pulmonary failure.

Number two had been struck by the same car when he went after number one. He was combative, which was not unusual in potential brain-damage cases, and was in restraints.

Number three, the policeman, had been hit by another car when he stopped to help. He had a broken leg and a broken toe on the other foot and was not part of Louise and Nancy's assignment.

When number two calmed down, they took off the restraints and moved him to the respiratory unit so Louise could do the blood work and get him intubated properly. Once there, he became disoriented and combative again, grabbed Louise by her wrist, and began to sling her around like a rag.

When Nancy came to help, he began slinging both of them back and forth like limp dolls. He was so strong they couldn't even keep their feet on the ground.

They were yelling for help, but they were being jerked around so hard their voices didn't have much volume. The unit was at the end of the hall, and no one could actually hear or see what was going on.

Louise's fingers were turning purple, but on one of her arcs back toward the head of the bed, she grabbed the nurse's alarm on the wall that signals a respiratory arrest, and everyone on the floor—doctors, nurses, X-ray technicians, lab people—rushed in.

By the time security arrived and got number two back into restraints, Louise was covered with sweat. Her pager had fallen off and been stomped by the man. Meanwhile, she had another patient waiting to return from CAT scan, and the woman with the spontaneous orgasms was still waiting in the ER, where they were getting annoyed that Louise hadn't come back for her.

"I still need the blood work on this man," a doctor said on his way out.

A few hours later, Louise turned into the driveway of her new home. As she parked, Walter came out the front door and took her in his arms and kissed her.

"How'd your day go?" he asked.

"Not bad," she said. "Kind of wild, but I'm home. I made it home."

THE PIECE of land that Walter bought had been a working farm but never a prosperous one. The land was gray and dense and an unusual mixture of sand and clay sometimes found in the piedmont of North Carolina. It retained too much water when it was wet and then dried out too fast when it finally did dry.

The old woman who'd been the last of the family to live there had died a few years previous, and the other family members had held on to the place, deciding what to do.

Eventually, they agreed to see how much they could get for the house and the land that most clearly belonged with it and to try to hold on to the remaining fifty-plus acres if they could get their price for the parcel they had decided to cut out.

The one-story house had metal roofing, commonly known as 5V for the five raised ridges on its face, which had been painted green at one time. Now it was faded. The first thing Walter did on the first cloudy day after they moved in was scrape the roof. It was not as steep as the one on which his father-in-law had used his mother-in-law as a counterweight, so he did not have to introduce their daughter to that side of marriage. It was in Walter's mind to bring the place back up and beyond what it had ever been.

He felt odd being home and coming out to meet Louise when she returned each day. He had some bitterness about all the work he'd put in at the housing agency and how he'd been treated and misunderstood and run over by the far right of the board of directors, even though statistically they'd been correct.

His parents had been out to the house, and though they would have normally been awkward and unappreciative of such a rural move, they'd been pleasant and even friendly. Since his marriage, they had changed toward him. The reason was, he thought, because Louise was so irresistibly loving and enthusiastic that they, in turn, when they'd never exhibited anything like those characteristics at all, became that way themselves.

Vincent and Dorothy had been over quite a bit, as the place was on their side of town, but farther out. They were still reserved with him in much the way that working-class people often are around people who seem different by virtue of education and money, but Vincent, trying to connect in some way with Walter, brought over tools and advice and Dorothy brought cakes, pies, and entire meals at times.

On the roof that day, with a can of green paint in one hand and a wide brush in the other, Walter saw Vincent's Buick turn in to their drive.

"It looks good," Vincent said, parking in the shade. "I took one of my sick-leave days today, that's why I'm here."

He looked at Walter for sympathy.

"Are you feeling bad?" Walter asked.

"Not too good."

"I'll come down and we can have something cold to drink."

"You keep on working. It looks good from back at the road. It'll be a treat for Louise if you finish up this side before she got home. You keep on going. I only wish I could help."

"Get a chair from the porch and sit in the yard while I paint," Walter said.

"I can't sit down."

There were two chimneys through the roof. One came from the kitchen up through the attic and out. The other, larger one was set between two bedrooms with two fireplaces. Both fireplaces had been bricked up by the time they bought the house, and one of Louise's dreams was to unbrick them and see if they worked. She hoped to have the one in their bedroom working by winter. What a scene, she thought, to fall asleep with a fire slowly burning down across the room.

"Does it go on okay?" Vincent asked.

"It soaks in too fast. A gallon's supposed to do four hundred square feet, but I bet it doesn't do half that."

The chimneys were flue-lined but were badly weather-worn on the outside. Both needed repointing. The flashing where they joined the metal of the roof was rippled and loose, and Walter nailed it back into the mortar joints before he repainted it.

"I'm only going to finish this side and then come down," he said, sensing Vincent was uncomfortable and bored. "Louise and I can finish it tomorrow."

"I wish I could help you. Me and Dorothy got a lot to do around our place tomorrow."

"It's all right. Don't even think about it. There's not much left, and it's my only job, for now, anyway."

"You know, as much as Louise worked with me all her life, I bet she's a pretty good helper."

"She is. She's better than me at a lot of things."

"I taught her all that. I treated her just like she was a boy in those ways. I reckon it didn't hurt her any."

The best way to paint 5V roofing was to paint the V first and force the paint in between the double Vs, then paint the flat between them. It wasn't difficult, but it was tedious and tiring.

"You missed a spot," Vincent said.

"Thanks."

"So, what're you going to do now that you quit building houses?" he asked. He never had entirely understood what Walter had done and thought it was something like being a contractor.

"I'm trying to figure that one out."

"It near about takes two incomes nowadays. Unless you got everything paid off."

He had no idea how much money Walter had, and Louise herself didn't know, though she thought there was enough. It was best, usually, not to let people know how much you were worth. It changed things.

Walter climbed down, put the brush in paint thinner, and then eased the ladder off the edge of the roof and onto the ground. Vincent came up to him just as he settled it against the house. He leaned close to Walter, as if he had to whisper something, even though no one was close by for acres.

Here it comes, Walter thought. He's been waiting since he got here to tell me.

"Mister," Vincent said, "I got it bad. Real bad. I'm hurting like you wouldn't believe."

"You got it again?" Walter asked, hoping to sound sincere.

"I just don't know what to do. It's nerves. I know it is."

"Yep."

"Can I use your bathroom?"

ONCE A WOMAN was crying or confused or weakened, there was less work for a man to do. Women had never understood this. Simply, it was easier for a man to want a woman this way. The connection between her being hurt or confused and his desire for her was odd.

"Actually, I don't feel like talking to you, mister," Mary said. "Get lost."

That's what one older redneck meant when he instructed a younger man on the job site: "The closer a woman comes to tears before bed, the closer she comes to coming once you get her there." It was simply easier to both accept and act on desire for a woman once she was weakened.

"Why don't you sit over there, bud," Mary said. "Way over there."

There was something so unsettling, so thoroughly unnerving about happy, spirited, passionate women that it was in the best interests of certain men to bring them down a little.

"Go find someone else. I'm not interested."

Women that aroused could cause a lot of trouble, and now that all women knew how to go that far and intended to, it was easy to see that, for this or that man, the problems were worse than ever.

"I was too busy for you the minute I walked in here," Mary said.

The mean-spirited concept of the scatterbrained woman shouldn't have been promoted and shouldn't have been allowed to continue once the neurological understanding was realized.

"What part of no don't you understand?"

Well-intentioned late-twentieth-century women made a big mistake when they imagined that sexual freedom, like knowledge, would liberate. They were wrong.

"Maybe you can't spell *no*. There're too many letters."

Their idea was a good one. Except for the earlier women whom the men cleverly boxed away by inventing the concept of the nymphomaniac, the new women thought their daughters should know the freedom and pleasure that they themselves had either not known or understood only late in life.

"I am sure, mister, that I do not know you. Absolutely."

Like many grand ideas, it seemed right at first and then it wasn't. Ironically, younger women and then even girls became enslaved to men in a way their mothers never had been.

"You don't know me, so take a walk."

Girls of high-school age and even younger now discovered desire so early in life that they made the terminal mistake of not hiding it from the boys like they used to. They would do anything for the boys, whatever they wanted. The pleasure they discovered, a substitution for the intimacy of the family they didn't have or for the coldness of the one they did have, was too much for them. They became enslaved in a newer, unexpected way.

"Get lost, or I'll call someone to get you out of here."

I know it's wrong, the girls would say, but I can't help

it. He has such a hold on me. He has such power over me. I'm just so lonely without a boyfriend. They would say these things.

"Where? When was that?"

There was once a high-school girl who thought she had become pregnant from slow dancing with a boy at the Christmas dance. Something sprung loose within her as they pressed against each other. She wasn't pregnant, but she was changed forever.

"You think I was there? I wouldn't know. I was so out of it that year, I don't remember anything."

Lately, in what might have been a curious trend had it not been so serious and widespread, many of the gals sought sanctuary with the lesbians, feeling they would be safer there.

"Oh, Lord. I guess that was me. Was that you? You're the one who took me home?"

The intellectualized equality that was promoted a few years ago was a mean promise that was made to the gals. It was a promise that could not be kept. Intimacy and pleasure and desire meant so much more to women than they did to men that the women were more lost than before.

"You have? Really? I can't believe you'd even remember me. I must have done something to make you remember me, huh?"

Sometimes, when marriage vows were spoken and the woman said I do, the fellow thought she had said I give. Heck, it was just the way the guys were brought up. Their mothers spoiled them rotten, enslaved themselves to them, waited on them day and night, hand and foot, and created the kind of monsters they themselves would have hated to marry.

"Darn if it isn't you. Now what was your name again?"

Mary Pristine had a glorious time that night. She hadn't had so much fun and laughed so much and been so relaxed and talked about so many different things in a year or two. She couldn't stop smiling as her old acquaintance followed her back to her house. She was deliriously happy.

Later, much later, exhausted and sweaty and about to fall asleep, Mary heard herself saying, out loud, I love you. The words simply came out. She hadn't planned to say them. They just spoke themselves as she lay sideways by him, looking at his magnificence and being overwhelmed by what they had done together and how he made her feel. I love you, she said.

KNOWING THE SADNESS of women had made Walter a different man, different from the one he'd been when he was young. Watching his sister and reflecting on the women he'd known, the ones his father had suggested he needed to leave alone, and reflecting on his mother's life, and how she had subverted herself to her husband and her family, though she had not seemed, at the time, to mind, and now watching Louise had caused him to be grateful that he had not been born a woman.

Because of this knowledge, it seemed to Walter right and it seemed honorable and unselfish to give a woman what it was she needed, what it was she desired, to make her happy. It was so easy to do once he had figured out that a woman wanted to be happy in a way that a man never even thought about or needed to be.

He could see, now that he was older, that past mistakes and excesses could cause a person to overreact later on. The people walking around with bottled water constantly in their hands and eating health food at a starvation or ascetic level had to purge their systems of the drugs they had taken before, the abuse they had put their bodies through, all the trendy sadism and cynicism they had been part of.

Strange, he thought, but fitting, that his father would

see anything between a man and a woman as the woman bearing the burden of weakness and the man prevailing and having his way. It was, for that generation, mostly accurate. The women gave those men the gift of submission. His father must have objected not to the presumed submission of the women in Walter's past but to the fact that Walter had not given them loyalty and care.

Louise arrived home. He watched her turn off the road. Seeing her smiling face made him smile when he hadn't yet that day.

"What's that sound?" she asked soon after coming inside.

"That?"

"Yeah, darling. That."

"It's something for you."

"You got me something? What?"

"Something that makes a sound like that."

"Come on. Tell me."

He brought out a young female Border collie.

"You got me a dog!" she screamed.

She took the dog from him and danced around the room while the collie, already alert and acting on her genetic mandate, swept the area with her gaze, looking for sheep, ducks, cats, or anything that might need to be tended.

"How did you know? How did you know I've wanted a dog for so many years? How do you know me so well already?"

"I took a guess."

"What's her name?"

"You decide that."

"But she's ours."

"She's yours."

"No, she's ours."

"She's my gift to you."

"Let me look at her little sweet face," she said. She studied him. "I'll call her Brownie."

"Sweetheart, she's black and white."

"I know, but for some reason, as we were looking at each other, and with that bandana around her neck, she looked like a little Brownie scout. Maybe it doesn't work."

"Brownie's fine."

"It's not. You're right. They're sheep dogs, so maybe we could call her something like Sheepy or Sheepish."

"Okay."

"No. You don't like that, either."

"I do. Whatever you say is fine."

"How about Smiley? Look at how crazily happy she is. Is that too stupid?"

"It's perfect."

They put a leash on Smiley and took her around their land to show her what would be the boundaries of her domain. Later, when she got used to where she was, they would let her run free, but by all that Walter had heard and from what the breeder told him, they should keep the dog inside or on a leash for at least a week, and maybe two, to let it accept this new place as home.

Together they cooked supper and then went on the porch, where Smiley was tied to a post. The steps leading up to the porch were rotting, and the base of the posts where they sat on the flooring was soft and in need of repair.

"There's a lot to do here," Walter said.

"I know. But won't it be fun doing it? Gosh. Everything seems like fun to me. Now."

"I've been thinking about something."

"Like what?"

"Like how it is I've been jerked out of what I was enjoying most of all, helping out people who need help."

"I know. I hate those men."

"I do, too. But they're everywhere. You have to figure out a way to live without having them in charge of your life."

"I know. We got the same thing at the hospital."

"I never have liked people telling me what to do when I knew what they were saying was wrong."

"You're so smart."

"It's only that I resent people who don't have the best interests of humanity at the heart of what they do or say."

"I love you."

"The board of directors was wrong."

"I believe you. Smiley believes you."

"But I don't feel right doing nothing about it."

"It's not worth causing trouble, is it?" she asked.

"No, I'm letting that go. But I want to do something to help the impoverished ways people have to live when whatever it is causes them to fail."

"Sometimes people bring it on themselves."

"True. But why? You see, I don't care about why it happens, only that it happens."

"Oh."

"Did Shirley bring that on herself?"

"Kind of."

"But we want to help her."

"Yep."

"Well, all this is leading up to what I've been wanting to tell you, what I've been thinking about lately."

"Tell me."

"I'm going to start a farming operation here that will grow vegetables, grains maybe, and later properly raise hogs or chickens, and I'm going to give away everything that we raise to the people who need it."

"Wow."

"And I want you to help me."

"I will."

"I've thought about it, and if we can just break even, and not deplete what money we already have, then that's all I want."

"Gosh, Walter, I never thought about you as a farmer."

"I lived with a friend for a year on a subsistence farm up in Maine once. I know something about it."

"Can you start now? Can you grow things in the fall? I don't think you can grow much, from what I remember of my parents' garden."

"You can start getting the land ready. I'm thinking maybe we might even have disadvantaged people work harvesting the crops when we need it. Maybe. Maybe they won't want to do that."

"I adore you, Walter."

"We might get a goat or two, also, I mean, right away."

"A goat? Weird. I never imagined owning a goat."

"I want to put them in that honeysuckle and kudzu and whatever else it is by the spring. That'd be a good way to clean it up."

"Smiley can look after them for us."

"So what do you think?"

"I think it's great."

"I'm going to call George, my friend who has the farm in Maine. I hope he and his family can meet you someday. They're going to love you. They're not going to believe I got lucky enough to find someone like you."

"I want to meet them."

"I feel like this is a good thing to do, that it'll work. I like everything about it."

Dorothy and Vincent had finished watching *Jeopardy,* and he was looking through the TV listings to see what else was coming on.

"Louise is so happy," Dorothy said.

"She seems to be."

"I'm glad for her."

"Me, too."

"Are you?"

"Of course I am."

"You don't seem to be."

"What are you talking about? Why wouldn't I be? Damn. Make sense, Dar."

"Well, I'm thrilled. It makes me feel good. It ought to make you feel good, too."

"Uh huh," he said, still looking through the paper.

"It makes me feel, I don't know, relieved. Freer. Something," she said.

"Uh huh."

Somewhere in the back of Dorothy's mind was the idea that she and Vincent should talk, that they could talk. There were always articles in the magazines about talking, but it seemed the women who wrote them didn't know Vincent or men like him. He only had a few subjects he could talk on: race relations, politics, sports, job gripes, diarrhea or gas.

"Do you know what I mean?" she asked.

"Uh huh."

"Right."

She felt as if she was going to have to get out of her chair and do something or else she might say something she was trying not to say.

"I know there're some things we can't think about."

"Yep."

"I don't mean those."

"Whatever."

"I'm going to the kitchen for a minute," she said.

She was of the generation of women who felt compelled to announce every move they were about to make to their husbands. They just did it, even though it often made no sense or didn't matter.

I think I'll sit over there, they might say. I think I'll go to the bathroom. I wonder if there's anything good in that magazine. I think I might read that book. I think I'll take my shoes off. I think I'll take my clothes off. I THINK I'LL TAKE MY HEAD OFF!

It seemed to Mary that the man had heard what she had said. She was almost sure of it. He had not actually been asleep, but at the sound of her words, he was as still as if he had found himself in enemy territory with a 60-caliber machine gun firing twelve inches above the ground. He stayed low. He never moved. He almost didn't breathe, she thought.

When he did, much later, Mary Pristine herself played dead. She watched him sneak out of the room. Standing naked beside the bed, in the dim light coming through the windows from the street lamps outside, he didn't look nearly as magnificent as she had thought.

Watching him roll his car down the driveway and delay starting it until he was in the street, she thought he didn't look too good at all.

For a minute or so, she thought that she was going to cry hard, so that the tears would pour down her face, over her cheeks, off the end of her nose, across her lips (those same lips that had just recently . . .) and off the end of her chin, onto her breasts (those same . . .), but she did not.

When Mary was a child, her family had one of the first remote-control television sets in the neighborhood. It was color, as well, something else unique.

Her brother, who without being aware of it prepared her for later life with men, was alternately kind and sadistic with her. He loved to lock her in the closet with no light, first gaining her trust, which was easily accomplished.

She would have done anything for him. He was almost like a god to her.

One day, shortly after getting the television and under strict orders not to use the remote, the use of which was reserved for their father after he got home from work, Walter picked up the remote and began to play with it.

Don't do that, she told him.

He pointed it at the television, and she tried to stop him again.

I'll tell Mom if you do.

Then he pointed it at her and told her that if she said another word or tried to leave the room, he would mash the mute button and mute her vocal cords for life, and she believed him, because somehow it seemed that he did have a power that she did not have. So she froze and stayed right where she was.

Now, years later, Mary was miserable. She found the bottle of Xanax and took two. She took the pills with a glass of wine. The notation in red on the bottle said not to take them with alcohol. Effects might be magnified.

Good. Great. Bliss me into twelve hours of sleep, she thought, and then she felt angry, really angry, because she didn't even know the man's last name again, because once more, just like before, it had been easier to believe that something miraculous was happening than to learn a man's name.

"I know you're upset to see the stitches," Shirley said, "but it'll be fine as soon as it heals. I'll put the bandage back on as soon as it airs out."

Manny was tired. When he was tired, it was best for

Shirley to be careful. He had been working on a landscape crew lately, and the bosses had him on the shovel while everyone else got to sit on the tractors or drive the trucks. This made him more irritable than usual, and Shirley understood this, having had jobs where she was treated unfairly.

"It's healing up nicely. There won't be a bad scar. You don't have to go back for stitches to be removed anymore," she told him. "They use something different now."

The new neighbors in Walter's house kept to themselves. They had not made any effort to meet Shirley or Manny, and Shirley thought it was best not to be in a hurry to meet them.

"Please don't be mad at me about losing the baby. The doctor said it was just all that I'd been through lately. I can have another one. Okay, Manny?"

Being tied to a pole and staring at a house in the early morning hours could cause a woman to want to forget everything about that house, since she had been put there to think about it until she realized what it was she had done wrong, because she didn't seem to know.

"Do you want to make a baby now, Manny? Do you?"

After the D&C, Shirley wasn't supposed to have sex for a few weeks. This kind of medical instruction merely showed how little doctors understood what went on between men and women.

"If you'll be real gentle with me, I know we can. Manny? Don't be cold to me. I love you."

One time Shirley and Manny had gone window-shopping. She had felt close to him and tried to take his hand. Won't you hold my hand? she asked. No, he said, but I'll slap you around a little if you want.

That was just the way some men talked. They just had

to talk that way, you see. It didn't mean they didn't love you.

"Isn't Smiley something?" Louise asked. She and Walter were looking at the dog in her cardboard box, where she had settled comfortably on a cotton blanket. "She's home. She loves it here, like me."

"I thought she'd be a good dog."

"She might bark, though, in the middle of the night."

"Talk to her, then," he said, "and tell her not to. I'm sure she'd understand you."

He knew Louise would take his words seriously. Louise was so tender toward every living being that she would take ants she found in the house and carry them outside and set them down, making sure they had a safe place to start over.

"I'm worried about Mary."

"Join the club," Walter said. "I've been worried about her for years."

"Let's have her over for supper this weekend."

Off in the woods an animal made a noise. Walter and Louise heard Smiley growl, but she never barked. The noise the animal made was like a human cry. Louise lay still and listened for it again.

"I wonder what that was?" she asked.

"I don't know."

"It sounded sad. And scared. Do you think it might have been a person?"

"Not likely."

"I've heard people make sounds like that. When they're in really bad pain, beyond hurting," she said.

"I think it was an owl."

Sometimes, at night, it was hard for Louise to stop thinking about what she saw at work. Assignment to the patients in the burn unit, or to the bone-marrow patients, or to the sad cystic-fibrosis patients was difficult. She usually needed to spend at least an hour with each one, four times per shift, and they cried and hurt and gasped and sometimes wanted to die. They couldn't sleep and couldn't eat, and it was hard to give them pain relief because getting IVs into them wasn't easy.

She remembered tonight, after hearing that cry and lying awake beside Walter sleeping, a seventeen-year-old cystic-fibrosis patient she had become fond of. The girl lived in Florida but had come to North Carolina for better treatment. She wanted to go to school so badly; but because she couldn't walk between classes, she had a home tutor.

The girl told Louise, when she had the breath to talk, that she wanted to go to Duke University. She had a 4.0 grade average, and as time passed and Louise saw her in and out of the hospital, she was accepted at Duke and even had a boyfriend.

The boyfriend was in a car wreck, and Louise ended up taking care of him, too. His family wanted all lifesaving measures done—chest compressions as needed, intubation on a ventilator—but he was miserable, pulled his IVs out, and died after three days.

His girlfriend died halfway through her freshman year at Duke.

Louise remembered how this girl always used to be sure she had a dark tan so no one could tell how blue her skin was, from lack of oxygen.

She was overwhelmed that night with how unfair it was for so much difficulty to be on any one person and how it could be that she herself was lucky and strong and healthy.

"Sweetie," she whispered, "are you awake?"

"Yes."

"How long have you been awake?"

"I'm not sure. I realized you were awake, and I woke up. What's wrong?"

"It's just that I really don't want to quit my job. I really don't. Please don't ask me to do that. I know you want me to help out on the farm, but don't make me quit my job."

Walter received a call from the new Homes for Humanity director, who told him a woman named Shirley was trying to get in touch with him.

Walter phoned her but the number was out of service. He drove to her house and saw that Manny's older model Grand Prix was not in the driveway. Had it been, he would not have stopped.

"Did they tell you I called?"

"Yes. I figured it had to be important, so I came right over."

"It is."

The house was even more bare than when Walter had first welcomed them into it. It seemed that some of the furniture, which, he guessed, probably belonged to Shirley's sister, was missing. There was still nothing on the walls.

"How's your new wife?"

"She's fine. How's Manny?"

"He's doing all right. He quit that landscaping job because, you know, it's getting on toward frost and there won't be much to do once winter comes."

He studied her face and her arms and her shoulders and all the other skin he could see, looking for bruises or marks.

"And you're not working?"

"No, I stopped."

"I did, too."

"Yeah. You're not with the agency anymore?"

"No. Louise and I are going to try something else."

"Jobs are tough."

"What's Manny doing now?"

"He's gone to look for a job."

"I see."

"He's been good to me, too. Remember I told you how upset he was that next morning. He's real sorry he lost it, I promise he is."

"I don't expect he'd be happy to see me here now."

"Well, no, but I just kind of had to get in touch with you."

"What's the trouble?"

"We need some money. I'm sorry to bother you with it, but there really isn't anyone else I could ask."

A tear started out of one eye, and she caught it with the top of her finger.

"What's happened?"

"We just have no money. We are completely out. Manny said the bossman cheated him on his last paycheck. I know I still owe you from last time, but could you just help me get through a few more days, just until he gets another job?"

In some way the help that many confused women needed was because of men, Walter thought.

Because of that, was it the duty of responsible men to help the women for whom life had gone bad due to other men? This was not as easy to decide as was, for instance, the abstract need of starving people or the circumstances of any distant, tragic soul.

Was it the duty of a man like Walter to still take care of women, to look after them and to undertake their rescue because he understood their weakness and understood that they were different from those of a man, understood that women could be undone by their own goodness? Was it right, always right, absolutely right, that he should be there for them when they failed?

"Sure," he said. "How much do you need?"

"A lot, actually."

"How much is a lot?"

"Six hundred dollars."

"Six hundred?"

"They're about to turn off the power. The phone's gone already. I'm sorry. It's just not been a good time over here, lately, and Manny's car broke down and he had to get it fixed."

"I don't have six hundred dollars on me."

"Can you give me a check? I'll cash it at your bank. They'll let me, won't they?"

If the faces of women were more sad now than ever, even though, as he had noticed before, they were more determinedly glamorous than ever, and if the desire of women was more obvious and impassioned than ever, and if the passion and goodness of women overwhelmed them and was different from what a man would ever know, then understanding this could only mean that the honorable thing to do was to be generous and compassionate.

"I'll write you a check," he said.

When Louise came home from work, Walter told her about Shirley.

"You did the right thing. I loaned a patient money once and knew I'd never see it again."

"It's not a lot of money. I also called a man and arranged to buy two goats."

"You did?"

"Yes."

"Goats are weird. I wonder if Smiley will get along with them."

The dog wagged her tail when she heard her name.

"She'll be in dog heaven with something to herd."

"I bet," Louise said.

"The fellow said these goats are pretty. They're an ancient Mediterranean breed and people use them for meat."

"Oh."

"He said the meat was sweeter and more tender than lamb. And less fat than beef or pork or lamb."

"So are we having goat meat for dinner?" she asked.

"How'd you guess that?"

"Are we going to tell Mary what it is?"

"Nope."

"How do we prepare it?"

"I've already got the cuts marinating, and then we'll bread them and bake them like pork chops. That's what they look like."

"Okay. Let's do it."

"You know, if it works out, we could supply this meat as a healthy alternative to beef, along with the vegetables, to the needy families."

"I like that. That's a good idea," she said. She was up for almost anything. It was that rich being married to Walter.

Mary and Louise took a walk around the farm. Smiley, who had easily learned to stay close to the house, slowly walked along with the two women. She had a spirited submissiveness to her that was endearing.

"We really are getting to know each other at a bad point in my life," Mary said. "I didn't use to be this pitiful."

"I don't think you're pitiful."

"I am. I don't know what it is. I've been single and dating men and having good times and bad times for years now, but lately I feel hopeless. I know things change. I know not to feel hopeless. I know what I'm doing wrong while I'm doing it and do it anyway."

"I'm like that sometimes."

"You got lucky with Walter. He's a little dry for my tastes, but he's a good man and he adores you and that's rare."

"He's not dry. I make him laugh all the time."

"I don't remember him as the laughing type. I used to make men laugh. They used to think I was the cutest thing they'd ever met."

"They still think it."

"But I don't care. I have my friends and I do my volunteer work and I fix up my house. At least, I used to."

"I love your house."

"You know what I do? I drink. I take pills to make me feel better, and then some more to make me sleep, and I sit around and worry. That's what I do."

"It'll change."

"I wish I had a job like you. You're so focused and happy. I can't get focused. I can't even sit still long enough to read a book. I read awhile, and then I start thinking about things I wish I weren't thinking about. Like, the other day I was thinking of how hard I'd tried to be normal all my life and how being normal comes down to having a family and children and a man, you know. There's always got to be the man there."

"Yep."

"I don't know what I want. Why is it I keep thinking I've got to fill in the blanks like, man, woman, children, house, and all that. Why do I keep going back to that?"

"Maybe you want it."

"I don't think so."

"I bet you do. You have a good heart."

"I hate my heart."

"No, you don't."

"Yes, I do. You haven't done the things in your life I have."

"I've done some stupid things."

"Don't tell Walter how blue I am."

"I won't."

"I know he doesn't respect me. I don't care. I hate the way Mister Perfect is always looking at me like the pathetic little sister who can't get her act together. I hate that."

"I won't tell him. And he doesn't think that anyway. He worries about you. He does. He worries about all kinds of things. He worries about women in general. It's kind of strange, but kind of sweet, too, but he thinks women have it so much worse than men, and it confounds him, I think, in a way that's kind of touching."

"I love it, Manny. Don't stop."

A man could get angry. This was known. Little things could make a man as angry as big things. One never knew what might set him off, but for sure he could get mad, and that was the way it was.

"That's nice," Shirley said. "Like that is nice."

Some women married young, and the man who got a young woman was lucky, for a while. In that first week of marriage when he threw the plate of eggs across the room because she hadn't cooked them right, she felt so bad. Why couldn't she make him happy? Why did she have to ruin his breakfast?

"Wait a minute, Manny. Wait."

If it wasn't the eggs, then it was the sandwich sliced the wrong way; it was the wrong brand of ice cream; it was the cookies that she had worked on all afternoon and surprised him with that first week of marriage, and he hates oatmeal cookies and she didn't know it? How stupid could she be?

"That hurts a little bit. Wait, would you?"

Sometimes, when a man comes home from work and sees a woman smiling, it's just common sense to question why she's so happy. What occurred in his absence to make her so happy? And what right did she have to be happy when he's so miserable, taking care of her and bearing all the responsibility on those broad shoulders she loves so much? There's something really stupid about a happy woman, like she's just too stupid to understand how stupid she looks walking around with a stupid smile on her face all the time.

"Manny, don't. God, Manny, please, that really hurts."

When a man is out of work, and he comes home from looking for a job, and his car isn't running well, and he's been treated like scum just because maybe he had a criminal record and maybe he'd been fired from the last job and he couldn't give that creep as a reference, and he walks in, and his woman knows things aren't going to go well, it's best for her to lie low and walk softly, do what he says, and don't look happy.

"No, Manny. I can't. I thought I could. I can't."

For a certain kind of man, anger and rage are all he has. They define his life. Take away the anger and the rage, and there's nothing there. Nothing.

"Okay, then. Go ahead. No, I'll be all right. I think."

Lacking anything else at all that he could do or be, he becomes angry, and the anger gives him power.

"What? Why'd you stop? What happened?"

If deprived of his rage, he can only limp along, like an oyster out of its shell, pale and weak and bitter.

"That? The check? Oh."

It's only natural that a man would suspect his woman of looking elsewhere for what he knows he can't give her. Anyway, any woman who'd do what he wants her to do in bed couldn't be a good woman.

"No. It's not that. I didn't do anything like that. It's for you. I swear."

Women are not to be trusted. If they'd do for one man, they'd do for any man, and besides, a woman who'd do the filthy things a man tells her to do couldn't be no woman he could respect.

"I don't think about him at all. Don't hit me. I didn't do anything. He didn't touch me."

You can tell when a woman has done wrong. She acts sweet and smiles too much and is a little too excited about nothing. She needs to learn how to be quiet and reasonable and decent, to have some dignity and honor about her.

Sometimes, it don't make no sense, but a woman who'll have sex with a man can't be no good. Not really.

"I don't want to see him. I want to be with you."

There aren't many good women left. They all dress like whores and act like whores, and it seems like they don't know how to be decent anymore, like they don't know how to say no to a man, and they ought to. A man respects a woman more when she tells him no.

"I guess that's where he lives. I'm not sure. I guess the address on the check is the new one. I promise, Manny, I don't know where he lives."

Poor Manny. He didn't understand what had happened. For a long time, women had been the guardians of moral restraint. Then they decided not to be and that made a mess of some of the men.

"Nothing happened. I swear. The money's just a loan

to help us out. It's nothing to him. He's got plenty. It's like five dollars. I swear. I don't want to go out there. I don't. I don't want to go out there. Please."

Walter had done a fine job cooking the goat. The rest of the meal was so tasty, too, and so full of that old feeling of nurture and family that Mary Pristine almost wept at the table, it felt so good to be with Walter and Louise, felt so wonderfully normal.

"Is this the way it was at home, when we were children? I don't recall it this way," Mary said. "I hated those sit-down meals every night."

"Maybe it felt this good to our parents," Walter said.

"I'm sure it did," Louise said. "But you haven't known family mealtime hell until you eat supper with my father," she said to Mary. "You just don't know the depths of embarrassment I would sink to."

"This is the tenderest pork I've ever had," Mary said. "It's so good. What did you put on it?"

"We marinated it for hours," Louise said. "That's the trick."

"I looked out the window and saw you two having one heck of a conversation," Walter said. "I wish I could have heard it."

"We were talking about you," Mary said. "I just shot down every decent thing she ever thought about you, Mister Perfect Brother."

"She did not."

"I told her about all the old girlfriends. I told her about the drugs and the drinking and that prison term—everything."

"None of that's true," Walter said to Louise, just in case Mary had told something she shouldn't have.

"She didn't tell me anything," Louise said.

"We did talk about Zephyry," Mary said.

"Who?"

"See. I told you he wouldn't know about it."

"This man they found who's got amnesia," Louise explained.

"Walter, don't you read the papers every morning like you used to?"

"Yes, I do."

"But he doesn't watch the six o'clock news," Louise said.

"And haven't you read about him?"

"I don't remember."

"That's just it. He doesn't either."

The phone rang. Louise got it. She put her hand over the receiver and told everyone it was her mother.

"Are they that bad?" Mary asked Walter. "I only met them briefly at the wedding."

"He is. He's a combination of good old Southern boy, hardworking husband and father, and someone who's cracked in a kind of benign but lunatic way."

"Can you get along with him?"

"Sure. Did you like the meat, by the way?" he asked.

"I said I did."

"It was goat."

Mary left at ten forty-five. It had been a good evening, and Walter and Louise felt wonderful, felt very much together, very married, very much partners in this new life. Less than an hour after Mary left, Louise was in bed and already blissed to an ever-higher level.

"I mean," she said, doing her now-routine giddy postmortem of their lovemaking, "it was like some kind of atomic bomb went off. Like I became atomic and vaporized myself. I'm gone. I'm not here. Wasn't it great?"

From his sleep he sensed she was talking, but he couldn't quite make it back to answer.

"This is all so new to me. I'm sorry. I just can't get over how great it is. Wow. Wait a minute. What was that? Is that the dog? What's that noise?"

In town, at the edge of the neighborhood where Walter owned the round house, were older houses that had been grand years earlier but were now apartments.

In one of these houses, which had a back stairway as well as a more formal front, lived Rob Wilmans, the part-time literature instructor who had dated Mary Pristine.

He had a bedroom, a living room, an upstairs sunporch that he also used as a sleeping porch, a kitchen, a study, and a bath. The rooms were furnished with antiques and paintings and collectibles he had gathered during the twenty-five years of life since college, and though he was a bachelor, his home was orderly and clean. Because it was autumn and the windows were open, the house was cool and fresh.

Rob was looking through a stack of old newspapers, trying to find an ad for a Miata he had noticed some time before. As he flipped through the sections, he paused on the wedding announcements when his eye caught the photo of someone he knew.

It was Louise. The picture was of her and Walter, with their wedding write-up beneath. He had not known she had married and had actually been planning to get in touch with her again.

He wanted to see her again not only because he had enjoyed being with her but because they had parted badly and he wanted to see if she would give it one more try. That she was married was a surprise to him, and a disappointment. He could not recall, of all the women he had known, a more willing, more daring, more unselfish and pleasing young woman than Louise. That she would marry so quickly after leaving meant that she was either pregnant or had changed a lot.

He looked at her picture and noted how she was dressed in virginal white. He wondered how well the man she'd married knew her. He wondered if she had left him for this man.

He cut out the picture and the announcement and laid it on his desk.

Lifting a dead body or a person who is unconscious is not an easy thing to do, even for a fellow like Manny.

A person's head sounds odd when it's hit hard from a solid blow or when that person falls onto her skull on the pavement. It's really kind of neat because it sounds like a cantaloupe at the supermarket when it's tapped to see if it's ripe. It sounds a lot like that.

A person can make unusual sounds if she's unconscious, if her airway is obstructed. She may make a bubbly noise, kind of like the sound a child makes when holding her breath under water at her first swimming lesson. She puts her face in and makes bubbles. It sounds like that!

Bubbling, then, and gurgling like a baby, Shirley rode in the backseat, which was doubly strange, because that was how she'd been riding in the same car when she and Manny first met, only the other man had been holding her down so she could not move.

Maybe if Manny had later looked back at how she had been dumped onto Walter and Louise's lawn, he might have realized the frailty of women and what an act of courage it was for them to give themselves to a man. Maybe he would have remembered the pleasure and companionship

Shirley had given him and how she had believed in him when the rest of the world had not and how good it felt to be good to a good woman and how much better it was to live with her than in prison.

Sometimes, though, a man could count on the infinite forgiveness of women if he could not change himself.

"There's something outside," Louise said.

"Where?" asked Walter.

"By the maple tree."

"You're right."

"Let's send Smiley out."

"She's too little to do anything."

He looked past her shoulders to what was in the yard, and at the same time they both understood that it was a body and that it was moving.

"Oh, no."

It was not easy for them to go out the door and look at this body. There was a fearfulness to doing so, similar to that of waking from a nightmare and opening your eyes, hoping that what you'd been seeing in your sleep was not actually in the room with you.

"I can't see the head," Louise said.

"Me neither."

"Maybe we should stay inside and call the police."

"Maybe we should."

Walter turned on the porch light and saw that the body had a pillowcase over its head. The hands were tied behind it and the legs bound at the ankles, and then he and Louise saw it was a woman.

"It's Shirley," he said.

Once outside, neither of them could get the ropes untied, they had been knotted so tightly.

"I'll get a knife," Louise said.

Walter was struggling with the pillowcase but had yet to free it when she returned and cut the cord that was holding it, as well as the ones holding her wrists and ankles.

When he pulled the pillowcase off, Shirley's eyes were wide and fixed, not comprehending him or Louise or where she was. She took a number of short, shallow breaths, which relieved Louise, and then realized where she was.

"I'm sorry," she said. "I told him not to bring me here."

"Can you walk? Can you get up?" Louise asked.

"I think so."

"Let me call the hospital and see who's there," she said. "We've got to take you there."

"I don't want to go."

Later, inside, Shirley sipped hot chocolate. Her hand on the cup, raised in the air to her mouth, was steady and did not tremble. This surprised Louise, who had given cups of coffee to people under stress many times, only to have to guide the cup to the lips to keep the contents from sloshing out.

"He's going to hurt me again. I know it this time. Can you get the locks changed on my house?"

"We could," Walter said. "I don't know how long it would take. I mean, they could. Homes owns the mortgage with your sister, so they could do that. I'll call later in the morning."

"Would a lock really stop him, if he wanted to get at you?" Louise asked.

"I guess not."

"You're right," Walter said.

"Maybe you should stay here," Louise said.

"No, I couldn't do that."

"You can."

"No."

"Do you have any family you could call?"

"Not close by."

"He knows she's here, anyway," Walter said.

"I'll go back after you change the locks. He probably won't do anything. He goes up and down. I'll just go on back."

"You know what?" Walter said suddenly.

"What?"

"She needs to stay with someone he doesn't know or have a clue about," Walter said.

"Then," Louise said, "how about Mary?"

A thunderstorm that had slowly been building broke over the house, and Smiley hid under the table, trembling.

"That's a good idea."

That same storm awakened Mary from the dream she was having, and she saw it was six-thirty in the morning. She parted the curtains and looked out the window and noticed the leaves that had not yet fallen that autumn were now in her yard and in the street and clogged together in soggy dams in the gutters.

She then remembered she was to keep the nursery at church that morning and realized what good luck she'd had to have been awakened by the storm, since she'd forgotten to set her alarm.

Although she rarely went to services, she had years earlier signed up to keep the nursery as a way to show her husband what an all-around woman she was and how much she loved children (even though she wasn't sure she did), and she had kept on even after he'd left.

The rain swept in against the windows, blowing from

the east, which would mean a lot of water coming off the ocean. She had once been caught in a storm in the twenty-six-foot sailboat she and Harris Benjamin owned and kept in a slip at Oriental, North Carolina. The weather came up so fast they couldn't get to shore, and try as they might, they could not keep the boat pointed into the wind and waves. They kept going sideways, and she was sure they would tip over. It was one of the most exciting times she could remember.

The boat was gone—he got the boat—and he was gone and the excitement was gone. She had caused all of it to be gone because she thought she needed even more excitement. What a stupid mistake she made and what remorse she felt for who she had been during those last couple of years with Harris Benjamin Calhoun, of the great and distinguished and respected and infuriatingly polite and genteel Calhouns of South Carolina, about whom she often wondered. What was the family like now? What were the brother and sisters doing? She also thought about how completely they had shut her out once she betrayed their brother, who himself had been something of a rebel, having had the audacity to have set up his law practice in his wife's state of North Carolina.

She ground her coffee beans and folded the filter and set it in the maker and poured in the hot water and thawed a sweet roll and had a glass of juice and sat at the table with the paper spread out, looking a lot like her husband used to look on Sunday morning, eating and reading while she sat in a chair nearby, studying him and waiting, in some sweetly perverse way, for him to call on her for something else, whatever he would want.

She showered and dressed and went to church and afterwards had lunch with some friends and then went home and retrieved the message from her answering machine and called her brother.

"Don't let her go back to him," he said quietly into the phone after he'd explained the situation, of which she knew some, having seen Shirley when she'd visited at Walter's round house. "She's already thinking she ought to let him know she's okay, that he didn't really hurt her. Can you imagine?"

"I can," Mary said.

"She wants to be sure he isn't suffering thinking about her being really hurt when she says she isn't. This worries me."

"It's a female kind of sickness, Walter."

"Will you talk to her? Will you keep her safe?"

"Sure. Bring her over."

Because Rob Wilmans had had the discipline and determination to have gotten his PhD in literature, he understood and valued the concept of research into a subject and had applied this effort into researching what it was women wanted in bed.

The research indicated women had a curiosity and need for degradation, although they denied it, and because his extensive research into this field was exciting to him, he had put many personal ads in the magazines and papers seeking "curious" women, women who wanted to explore their sexual curiosity.

Little did those who responded know that Rob already had plans for them according to his own stunted and cross-eyed curiosity. The surprising thing was how many women answered his ad, although some of them were looking for an easier way to make money than on the street.

He had not met Louise this way, however. They had met while she was a student in a night-school course he was teaching in composition. He had discovered that this particular course was a gold mine of women who wanted to better themselves and especially of women who were impressed by his credentials and learning and how it could be possible that a man as sophisticated as he could be interested in working-class girls like them.

Louise was way above the average in women he had met this way, he thought, looking at the wedding photo he had kept. She had seemed interested in him in some fearless and daring way that was new to him. Most uneducated women, he had found, were easy marks for the seductive effects of long conversations, a lot of eye contact, attention, and sympathy, as it seemed they got little of that from their usual type of man.

Louise had, he recalled, met him eye to eye and toe to toe, and she had thrilled him in a new way that he wished he could have continued on with, had she not broken it off with him, now, it seemed, as he thought about the time and circumstance, when she had met this new man, who then quickly became her husband.

He was quietly infuriated that she had broken it off so quickly. He had entertained a few ideas over time when she refused to return his phone calls or answer his letters, ideas not of getting even with her but of getting her back into his life or, at least, into his bed a few more times. He had in mind things yet to do, and Louise was his woman of choice for these ideas, which, he might have added had anyone questioned him directly on the subject, the research fully supported.

M ARY STOOD outside the bedroom door and listened to Shirley talking on the phone. After a few minutes
of not being able to hear the words clearly, she went down-
stairs. Shirley came down soon after.

"I finally got him," Shirley said. "I know you didn't
want me to call him, but I had to. I know I shouldn't
have. But I had to. Thank goodness they reconnected our
phone."

"You shouldn't have done that. I hope you didn't tell
him where you were."

"Well, I had to or how else could he pick me up? He'll
be here in a few minutes."

Mary debated what she could say to this woman, who
was too obviously screwed up to understand anything reasonable. She debated whether she should say anything at
all, given the embarrassingly doomed optimism of this
woman in front of her.

"I wonder if that was a good idea," Mary said. "Sometimes, you know, it does a man good to let him stew in
his own juices for a while."

"Yeah, I guess so. But when I talk to him, he's just so
sad and sorry sounding. And I'm not as crazy as you're
thinking, and I can tell you are thinking that. I held out

for what I wanted, and I got it. He swears he's going to counseling with me tomorrow, and he swears off the alcohol for good."

"Oh."

"You know, it's not him. That's something we both understand now. It's the alcohol that does it."

"Oh."

"Everything's going to be all right now. I mean, slowly it will. You just don't know him like I do. You don't know his heart and how bad he wants to do right."

"Okay."

"Don't look at me like that."

"I'm sorry."

"I've been here before. After he does something like this, he'll do anything for me."

"It's just that I thought you hated him. Walter said you said you hated him."

"I hated what he did last night. I would never say I hated him."

"Oh."

"Listen, Mary. You've been married, right?"

"Yes."

"And did you ever say you hated your husband?"

"I guess so. I may have said I hated things about him."

"And have you ever wished you had him back, now that he's gone? I bet you have."

CHAPTER 28

THE RESEARCH indicated that until recent times the arcane understanding of the arousal of women was unknown to men. Later, it became clear that the mandarin use of language applied. Once this was known, and the key to what had been previously closed to men could more easily be opened, the manipular aspects of female desire could be better controlled.

The symbolic state of menstrutam, therefore, could be attained, and the solid, previously immutable substance that was the woman and her desire could be dissolved. I have melted, she might say, or you have dissolved me, and I am yours.

The research, Rob Wilmans remembered, also indicated that married women had affairs, and lots of them, and it also revealed that these women, when persuaded to go against their will, had the potential for unusual passion. To become degraded in their own eyes and in their husbands' was, the research showed, a part of the curious sexual experience of women.

"May I speak to Louise?"

If being a party to the visual experience of the passionate act meant little or nothing to a woman and to her arousal, then why, it could be asked, would any woman agree to be videotaped? What would it mean if she agreed to that?

"This is Walter."

What if she did not agree? What if the videotaping were done in secret? That should be against the law. It's not. Laws do not need to be written to protect women. They can take care of themselves now that they have the same knowledge as men.

"She stayed home from work today? Of course. I forgot. I'll call her at home. Thank you very much."

Sometimes, later in life, older women were surprised by their desire. It had not been known to them earlier. This was, in some ways, fortunate, as these women had been spared the predatory uncertainty of passion. It was fun, though, really nifty fun, for a guy to get hold of one of these women who didn't know what she had waiting inside her and bring it out.

The young women, the research showed, knew what was waiting for them, and they went toward it like moths to a light. Singed, they came back for more.

"What do you mean, is this really her husband? How dare you talk to me this way."

A young Japanese or Chinese woman was lots of fun for a man. Often brought up to be subservient, they became enslaved, the research revealed, not only to the man but to their passion, as well. That was nifty fun, was it ever!

Desire, study had shown, at the level women now understood it, was not a universal phenomenon, but was more a function of temptation and the sly and zealously crafted elements of arousal within the culture, which made it not uneasy to reach the spontaneous orgasmic state, which, though embarrassing, many of the women learned to live with, conceal, to some degree, or disguise in the manner that some people learn to disguise a tic or a hacking cough, with a laugh or a sweep of the hand.

This was only one level of the study of women.

But what about love? In fact, Rob Wilmans had accidentally fallen in love with Louise, with her abandon, with her sweet and tender heart, with her courage and spirit, and with her rejuvenating sense of humor, which gave him a smile when he was with her. The research hadn't explained that at all.

What more than annoyed him was that she had changed the rules on him after initially agreeing to them. That made him resentful and full of a troubling vengeance. She had left him without a word and had refused him in a way that he was unprepared for. Women, for the most part, did not walk away so easily and quickly from men who made love to them.

It didn't have to be this way, Rob thought. Seeing Louise again and knowing her in the way he used to would go a long way in, how should one say, abrupting the feelings that he had thought he'd negotiated well—until he saw the picture in the paper.

Now and then, in a person's earthly tenure, a vision of how life was meant to be comes clear. When the luck is good, there is another person with you who sees that vision and understands it in the same way as you.

For Walter, that person was Louise, and now for her, it was Walter, and this day spent together working on the farm with their future so visibly in sight was more than special. It was a rebirth for Louise, away from sadness and exhaustion and fear, and back to hope and laughter.

"Did I tell you about the old couple a few years ago who came into the hospital from being in a wreck?" she asked.

"I don't think so."

"She was driving and she asked how is it on the right?,

and he said no on the right, and she thought he said go on the right, so she pulled out in front of a car. They were still arguing about that, lying side by side on separate tables. Still arguing about it."

"I believe that," he said.

"It sounds like something my parents would do."

"Yes."

The trees on the property remaining with the farm encircled the open land. The house was in the middle, so that, seen from above, it was a dot in the center of a circle formed by open land, which was then a smaller circle within a larger one consisting of the forest. These trees were like a quiet, sturdy fence around the life within, and it was under one of these mature hardwoods that Louise and Walter sat, on high ground, looking back across the fields and toward their house so that they themselves were seeing where they lived, and, in a sense, how they lived, and what they now were, from the distance that others might see them.

"It's lovely," she said.

"I know it is."

"You found this place. I'm grateful to you for that."

"We found it. It was you I wanted to find it for."

Across the field and inside the house, the phone was ringing. Smiley heard it ringing, but they did not. The machine answered. Walter's voice gave the greeting. Then it was time for the caller to speak.

What does an ex-lover say to a machine with his ex-lover's new husband's voice standing at the gate like a guard, forcing him to go through the husband's firm commands so that he could get to the woman he knew first.

He leaves a message that will confound and annoy, one that only the woman will understand. He says, without introduction, "If a body meets a body coming through a lie," and then he hangs up, leaving only the bombastic and referential word play to consider.

The next day Louise returned to work, and Nancy met her as she came in the door.

"Someone called for you yesterday," she said.

"Someone called here?"

"Yes, and he said he was Walter, but he wasn't."

"He wasn't?"

"You know who it was, don't you?"

"I do?" Louise asked, as if asking herself if she did, unable to think clearly enough to evade the question properly.

"Listen to me, Lulu. You know I know who it was. You know I can guess. It's Rob."

"Yeah. He called here before. I hung up on him."

They couldn't talk long. The shift before them had left a lot of work, which now fell on Louise, Nancy, and the rest of their crew. Someone should have been sent on transport from the respiratory unit a half hour ago.

"I'll go, I guess," Louise said.

"You better not. As a matter of fact, you better be careful what you do. You look out of it."

"I'm so worried. He left a message on our answerphone. I got it before Walter heard it."

"I'm going out on transport. Get some coffee, and try to get clear and be careful."

"All right. Thanks, Nan. I'll be fine. I'm a pro. I can do it."

"I know you can."

"God knows, I've done it a million times when I thought I couldn't."

Before Nancy returned and almost before Louise could

orient herself to being back, a call came in for her, and she was told it was important. She paused only a moment before deciding, much as she would decide often every week when something difficult or unpleasant had to be done with a patient, that she would face it down, she would talk to Rob, if it was him.

"I love you," he said. It was the very first thing he said, without even identifying himself or saying hello.

He knew these words were the right ones to say. The research had revealed that these words had a power over women they did not have over men and that a woman had the ability to believe the words even as the man saying them was cutting her in half with a dull saw.

"I love you," he said.

The words were such a violation of who Louise was then and of who she was with Walter and of what they had together that she did not have any response ready.

"I need to see you."

"I'm married," she finally said.

"I don't care."

"Don't ever call me again here. Don't ever call my home."

"I'll do more than call it if you don't agree to see me."

She hung up. The phone rang again immediately.

"This is Walter," Rob said.

"Don't call me again."

"But I am Walter. I am your husband. I am your true husband, and I was before he came along."

"I'll call the police if you don't leave me alone."

"I wouldn't do that. I'd think about that once more."

"I will."

"Think about your spouse and what he might think about you if he knew what I know, or if he saw what I've seen, something that you didn't know existed."

She hung up again. She went to the bathroom and forced herself not to cry, to calm down, and to go back to her patients.

She only made it to lunchtime before she began to fail. She told Nancy about the calls. She told her she was having trouble concentrating.

"You go home, then."

"I can't go home."

"Sure you can. I can cover for you."

"I can't let Walter see me this way."

"Then go somewhere else and figure out what to do."

"I can't ask you to cover for me."

"Hey, who are you talking to? I can do this whole unit alone if I have to. Okay? Take off the whole week if you need to. I won't even work up a sweat. You look after yourself now."

Louise told her supervisor she felt too ill to work, and Nancy assured the supervisor that she could handle the load remaining, and then Louise took the elevator down to the parking lot.

As she got into her car, she thought of the one person she could talk to, someone who not only would understand but who might have been there herself.

Mary Pristine was looking through the classified ads in the employment section.

I've got to do something, she had told herself.

She realized that she had been sitting around almost four years waiting to either get married again, fall in love again, or have something happen to her, and nothing had. She didn't expect to actually find a job by reading the classifieds, but she was looking through the ads to find out what kinds of things people did.

Since she didn't need the money, the question was more what might she do that she could enjoy rather than what might she do to merely survive.

"You don't look too good," Mary said as she let Louise inside.

"I'm in trouble."

Mary could not have been more surprised to see Louise here, unexpectedly, saying that she was in trouble and looking as frightened as she did, than if her ex-husband had returned and proposed marriage.

"Is it Walter?"

"No. Of course not."

"You better sit down. Let me get you something cool to drink."

Louise began to tell her about Rob Wilmans and how she met him while taking a night-school course and how she began to be interested in him.

"I was messed up back then. I was just a mess."

"But you're so calm and levelheaded," Mary said. "It seems to me that you've always got to have been this way. Your whole life looks steady and balanced."

"I didn't know he was crazy when I started with him. I mean, I just didn't know. How do you know? How do you know a man's insane until he lets you know it, and he was good at getting me to do what he wanted and to think the way he was thinking, and I hate myself for that."

"I understand that. I do."

"And now it's like he thinks he can again. What am I going to do?"

"We'll think of something."

"Walter will leave me if he finds out about Rob. He'll leave me."

"No, he won't."

"And I'll deserve it. I'll deserve anything he does to

me. I'm no good. I let Walter think something about me that wasn't true."

"You let him think you were what?"

"That I was naive. That I never dated. That kind of thing."

"But we all do that. That's what they want to hear."

"I took it further. It seemed like he wanted it to go further."

"Well, I have to tell you something now that's going to make everything even crazier."

"What?"

"I know Rob Wilmans. I've been with him."

"It can't be."

"Oh, yes. As a matter of fact, when you began to describe him and how he was, before you even said his name, I knew who it was."

"Oh, Lord."

"I think I may have been who he saw soon after you and him broke up."

"We didn't break up. There wasn't anything to break up. I just never showed up again. It wasn't like I loved him. I never told him I did. I don't think I ever did."

"I feel so sorry for you. He would prey on a young woman and get her tangled up in his ugliness. He doesn't get far with women his own age, I can tell you that."

"I have nothing but bad memories of him. I was sick. I must have been sick."

"I've been there."

"I'm so ashamed."

"I know. I know what you mean."

"Why did I let myself be that way? Why? I'm not that way. I'm not."

"I know you're not."

"I swear I'm not. I never enjoyed anything we did. You've got to believe me. I didn't."

"I believe you."

"I knew everything about it was wrong."

"Of course you did."

"I did. I just didn't know how to stop it. I couldn't have enjoyed being with him. I just couldn't have, could I?"

"It's complicated, Louise."

"Oh, Lord, the nights I spent there. He used to get so disgustingly drunk he'd throw up in the middle of the night. I'd wake up and he'd be throwing up on me and the bed and I'd have to clean up. Now why—" she started to say, but Mary finished the sentence for her.

"—didn't you just leave, just walk out the door and leave him in his own puke?"

"Yes."

"I would have thought you would, knowing you as I do. That's the kind of thing I'd have thought you'd do."

"I was sick and I was screwed up, and now Walter's going to find out."

"Young girls attract these kind of men. It's a given. It wasn't your fault."

"Why does he call me and tell me he loves me? Why? He doesn't and never did. Did he? How could he?"

"He loves himself. Forget the rest."

"And the tape. Oh, Lord," Louise said and cried again. "I didn't know he was doing that. I swear I didn't."

"Well, the thing right now is to get yourself in better shape and go home just like you've been at work and don't let on. Chances are Rob won't do a thing. And I'm going to be figuring something out in case he does. But first, protect what you have with Walter and don't let on."

"He'll see through me."

"He won't, but I know my brother and I want to tell you something. Even if he found out, he'd love you just the same."

"No, he wouldn't."

"He would. But he won't find out, so just buck up some way. Go home and be normal and pray. Pray like mad."

Louise composed herself on the drive back to her now-not-remote-enough farm. Phone numbers could be found out. Addresses were more difficult to find, but not that difficult.

She called her mother at a pay phone just before she left the city limits.

"Just don't give him any information," she said to her mother, who was alarmed. "If he calls, hang up. Tell him I told you to hang up, if you can't do it any other way." Then she added, "And don't tell Dad anything." Then she realized he would have to know, too, if he were to deflect the calls, as well. "Tell him, I guess," she said, "but make it sound like just a little nuisance, which is all it is, really, Mom, okay? I just don't want to talk to the guy or have him know where I live, okay?"

She entered her house with a spring in her step so energetic it looked as if she'd bounced off a trampoline and shot through the doorway and into Walter's arms.

"I sure did miss you," she said.

"I missed you, too."

"Boy, I had some day. If I seem a little out of it, don't worry. All kinds of stuff happened. Nancy went out on transport, and the stupid driver got lost on the way back, and then it took so long for them to get back, she ran out of oxygen for the patient, but that turned out all right, after they did get in, and then all kinds of other things, but hey, I'm home, and tell me everything that happened with you, and how are the goats and how's old Smiley here? How're you?" she asked the dog, then caught her breath while Walter momentarily basked in the wonder of such a greeting, before looking more closely at his wife and thinking there must be some reason for it.

"All right," he said, "what is it?"

"I'm only glad to be home is all."

"What've you done? That look on your face is a dead giveaway."

"It is? For what? I mean, there's nothing."

"You've bought something?"

"No."

"You've bought me a truck."

"No, but I will. I'll give you one for Christmas."

"You're pregnant."

"No, but I'll be that, too, if that's what you want now. Is it? I thought you wanted to wait."

"You got a raise?"

"There's nothing, darling, nothing."

A ritual has its own force. It has a comfort. It has a familiarity and a history that seem to be necessary. There would have been a reason for the ritual to begin.

Dorothy served supper. It was the right thing to do. She'd been doing it since before Louise was there to enjoy it, since before she was born. The food always tasted the same. It was familiar. It was a comfort.

"Thanks, Dar," Vincent said. "You sure can cook."

A man came home from work and became content. The children were still. There was the hope of sanity and closeness and appreciation.

"I love sweet potatoes. I love them with butter," he said.

There was the chair in front of the TV. The chair reclined and the footrest popped out, and this was luxury to some men. This and all the rest of the house that was his home.

"I know you do," she said.

Louise and her friends didn't understand how simple it was to please a man, how it was not necessary to be everything to him. This was where the young women went wrong. They had to leave something for themselves. They went too far in giving themselves and in expecting their lives to become glorious and exalted through the skin of men.

"How about something different tomorrow?" Dorothy asked.

"Like what?"

"Like stir-fry," she said, picking something out of the air she had never made. "Like a vegetarian stir-fry," she added, knowing what his answer would be.

"Good God, no," he said. "Don't be thinking like that."

Recliners were easier to transport now. The La-Z-Boy company had developed a way to separate them into two pieces so they would fit into the backseat of the average man's Buick or Mercury. Then, if the old recliner broke, a fellow could zip down and get another one right away to replace it. It was part of the ritual.

"Uh-oh," Vincent said, sniffing the air and trying to figure out in the most concerned and curious and thoroughly sincere manner what had come out of his body, "that's them sweet potatoes, I bet. Damn if it isn't."

Dorothy stared at him without speaking.

"What's wrong with you?" he asked, as if she could

doubt him, who, if there was ever one awarded, would be the winner of the Nobel Prize for bodily emissions research.

"Me? What's wrong with me?"

Rob Wilmans, teaching another evening college course, parked his newly acquired Miata convertible and walked to his classroom. He wore Gucci loafers, triple-pleated pants, a silk shirt, and a large bow tie, which was his trademark.

The course he was teaching was an introductory creative-writing course, and the data showed that there was a greater chance of finding innocent and "transitional" women in this course than in almost any other. The data also indicated that women liked a clean-looking man who dressed with care, spoke politely, conversed at length on multiple subjects, and drove a natty car.

The data indicated that catching a woman in the transitional phase of her life—that is, when she had left a long relationship or marriage and wanted to prove herself to a new man—could be more than rewarding. A transitional woman would do anything for the new man.

The data, which could be properly pronounced as "dada," corresponding to the art movement, or as "date-a," at least in the research he had read, allowed that a woman leaving a long and unhappy marriage in which she had shared the conjugal bed actively with a man she neither ("ni-thur") loved nor respected, a woman leaving this kind of marriage was a marvel on the sheets and would do anything and everything to prove what a lively lass she really was.

To the adverse (archaic usage, but acceptable), some women were gems of delight, and thrilling beyond what most men would ever experience, and finding one of them would cause a man to want to keep her for himself. This is how Rob felt about Louise and why he was so astonished and annoyed to see that she had quickly married. To be deprived of her sweet company saddened and angered him.

Obviously, he was aware of the correlations between anger and sexuality. Women in the early stages of an affair often mistook anger-driven sexuality—that is, activity that is urgent, insistent, and mildly to severely brutal—for love and affection, though they soon learned what it was all about once they used the word *no* for the first time.

With Louise, Rob had risen above this, and he missed her the way a person misses home, once away from it. He longed for how she made him feel.

There was thunder again, and Smiley left her bed of blankets in the corner of the kitchen and flew through the living room door and landed on the sofa beside Louise and Walter.

"She's going to want to sleep with us tonight," Louise said.

"Yes, but she's not going to."

"Aw. Please?"

"Nope. She's got to learn thunder won't hurt her. She can do that."

Louise had a glimpse of children in her life then and the role of the man to hold the line, to understand and sensibly enforce practicality, to keep the woman's tender heart from gathering all the children and dogs and cats and rabbits and guinea pigs and turtles picked up off the road and birds with broken wings, to somehow keep all of them from piling in their bed every night, the way a good man will understand the limits of how far you should go, knowing that going too far was wrong, that letting desire rule your life would not work. A good man understood how far desire should go.

"We're going to have a great life," she said, imagining then the order of her life, having kissed the children good night after a glorious evening, having played Monopoly together and laughing, and then the children were asleep with angelic faces and their pure lips parted in the sweet movement of air unobstructed and she and Walter were in their own bed, where they talked about the day and about life and the future and made plans, then made love and slept soundly. It was easy to see that, to imagine it. She would have to be certain that it came true, that nothing from her past ruined it.

"Yes, we are," he said.

The storm continued far away after Walter and Louise went to bed, and in the middle of the night, he had to lock Smiley in a closet to keep her from scratching up the bedroom door, trying to get in to them.

At the same time, Dorothy watched her husband sitting at the kitchen table, staring at the slice of pie she'd saved for him. The fork was resting on the plate with the prongs just touching the sweet, dark syrupy filling under the pecan topping, and her husband's hands were on either side of the plate. The crust, which she'd made herself as she always did, was fluted and rose above the back edge of the pie like a crown. It was perfect and delicate. Had Vincent merely tapped it with his fork, it would have broken off in crisp flakes.

"I don't want this damn pie," he finally said, taking it to the trash can. "I don't want the little piece of pie you baked for someone else," he said, "and saved one little piece for me."

He stepped on the lid opener and dumped the whole thing into the plastic bag. "I'm sick of getting the left-overs."

She looked down and said nothing.

"The leftovers of a pie. To hell with it."

In the morning Walter had an appointment to look at a used tractor and some equipment. Just before he left home, Louise called from the hospital and reminded him that she loved him.

He loved her, too. He also wanted the farming idea to work. It would be wonderful to be able to be a part of the world only in the way he wanted to be, only when he wanted to be, and not to be part of the corruption that seemed to govern even the best-intended efforts. The more time he spent thinking about the farm and the good work he could do with it, and the more time he spent with Louise, the more he realized what an island of purity of thought, deed, and intimacy he had lucked into.

The tractor was a John Deere 2020. It came with a small chisel plow, a rotovator, a bottom plow, a harrow, a two-row planter, a scrape blade, a grain drill, and a sickle bar mower. The man also had an older one-row John Deere 430 with a set of underbelly cultivators.

Though Walter knew nothing about farm equipment, it was just one of the new things in his life he would have to learn, have to master, have to become good at, as he tried to do with everything else that came his way.

Because he had always done well, and because he had, always, been able to see the truth behind every facade and because he wanted his life with Louise to be as unobstructed by fear and doubt and misconception as was humanly possible, when he returned from getting the equipment, but before it was delivered, he phoned his sister.

"I'm worried about Louise," he said. "She's changed a little. In the last couple of days, something's happened."

"Really? Like what? Like how?" Mary asked.

"I don't know. She seems worried in a way she's not been before."

"Have you asked her about it?"

"Sort of. I haven't said much. I don't want to seem paranoid if there's no reason to be."

"I just don't know."

"I wonder if it's her work. It seems too much for her at times."

"It could be."

"Or could it be, and I hate to think it, that she's unhappy being married, because that's all that's changed."

"I'm sure that's not it. She adores you and adores her life, so forget that."

"But what else has changed?"

"I don't know."

"Maybe it's me. Maybe I'm guilty of being like her father and don't know it. Maybe I'm oblivious to treating her in some bad way and don't see it. I don't want to be that way. I don't think I am."

"You're fine."

"I wonder if starting up this farm has done it."

"I doubt it. Do you want me to talk to her, to see if I can find out anything?"

"No. Don't do that. Don't even tell her I called."

Louise did her rounds and found that the shift before hers had left things in good order.

"I'm sorry about yesterday," she said to Nancy. "I know better than to let personal problems interfere with my work."

"Yeah, sure, like we don't? Come on, Lulu, it's nothing."

"Well, thanks for covering for me."

"Anytime."

"I'm so worried. About you know what."

"I know. I'm worried, too. He never was any good."

"The thought of ever seeing him again repulses me," Louise said.

"I wish he'd end up in here. I'd fix him," Nancy said, "and no one would be the wiser. Just a natural death."

Later that day, Rob called. Louise refused to take the call, so Nancy talked to him. He spoke softly and seemed reasonable and said that he merely wanted to understand what had happened to him and Louise, that he just wanted a meeting to find out, to put things to rest.

"Bull," Louise said. "When I walked out on him, he acted like he didn't care."

"I don't know about that. I'm just telling you what he said."

"I hate him. I hate him so."

"He said if you didn't talk to him next time he called, he'd meet you after work, and if you wouldn't talk to him then, he'd call your house until he got you."

"Oh no."

"So I said maybe we could, together, me and you, meet him somewhere. It kind of seemed like the best way to defuse it all, you know? Okay?" Nancy asked. "Did I do right?"

Louise and Nancy were sitting at an outdoor table at a bakery and were wearing coats on the cool day when Rob arrived in his Miata with the top down. He was dressed once again in his signature bow tie, baggy, pleated pants, and expensive loafers.

"Lord," Louise said, "I think I'm going to be sick."

"Hang in there," Nancy said. "Let's just get it over with."

He walked toward them with his nose ever so slightly up in the air and scanned the crowd as if he couldn't find them, then acted startled when he did see them.

"So," he said. "We finally meet again."

She was doing her best not to give him the satisfaction of seeing how upset she was. She didn't want to talk for fear her voice would betray her.

"I told Louise what you said, and we're only here to ask you to stop calling her."

"Is that what you want, Louise?" he asked with a pained voice, as if the hurt she had done him had practically killed him and he could barely make himself heard.

"Yes, it is," she said clearly.

"Of course, I understand that you're married. It's that it was so sudden, I was taken off guard. I only want to ask you what I did wrong, and perhaps this is something you don't want to discuss in front of someone else," he said.

"I'll leave."

"Stay," Louise said. "Nancy can hear anything."

"Then tell me what happened."

"I had to leave is all."

"But you owe me the courtesy of an explanation. You really hurt me. I did love you, you know. I do, actually."

"Don't talk like that to me," she said.

"I've been so lonely since you left."

"I doubt that."

"But I have. I thought we had something special. I thought we had a future."

"We didn't have anything, and you know it, so cut the crap and quit putting on an act."

"This is no act," he said, even more softly so that the women had to lean toward him to hear. "You seem to have anger in your voice, and I don't understand that. Did I do something? Tell me if I did."

"Look, I'm here to tell you to leave me alone. I'm happily married, and you have no right"—she said and then nearly did begin to cry—"to intrude into my life. No right at all."

"And you," he said, and touched his heart with his hand, "had no right to leave me so coldly."

"Oh, man," Louise said. "I can't believe this."

"You look wonderful, by the way. Marriage does suit you."

"Look, I'm not going to sit here and listen to this phony crap from you. Don't talk about my marriage. Don't talk about how I look. It has nothing to do with you."

"It did, once."

"I left you because I hated you, and I hated you because you used me horribly and you know it, and you took advantage of me and you know that, too."

"I don't recall it that way."

"It was that way."

"And then you married so fast. It hurt me so when I saw it. It was almost as if you'd done it to hurt me even more."

"Are you out of your mind? I married because I fell in love, okay? Now what else do you want to hear so you'll leave me alone. There is such a thing as harassment."

"Yes," he said, reflectively and softly. "And there is such a thing as video," he added, looking away and up toward the heavens, frowning, as if he had only just then thought of something.

"Video what?" Nancy said.

"Video whatever," he said.

"What video?" Louise asked. "Exactly what video?"

"I don't know anything," he said, his voice almost a whisper. "And yet, I know everything."

"Yeah, I remember that kind of talk."

"I shouldn't have said that. Nancy, it would actually be good if I could talk with Louise privately. How about it? It would be better."

"Go ahead," Louise said. "It won't take long. It's okay, really," she said to Nancy, who questioned her with her eyes as she left the table. "Really."

"Louise, I'm a rational man. I'm trying to be rational with you."

"Then leave me alone."

"Don't you want me to be reasonable?"

"I want you to understand, like I thought you already did, that it's over and been over and never was."

"I want you to be reasonable with me."

"I am married, for God's sake," Louise said, this time with tears in her eyes she could not hide. "Stay out of my life."

"I think about you a lot. I remember how we were," he said, and nodded, as if remembering once more. "And I want to tell you I've spent many nights alone thinking how you left me when we were so good together."

"Are you finished?"

"No."

"I am."

"If that's so," he said softly, "then I might be forced to make you pay for the pain you caused me."

"You're nuts. You're crazy as hell."

"I told you once I made a video of us. I told you and you refused to believe it, but it's true. I did do it."

"You go to hell," she said. "I'll kill you if you did that."

"No, you won't."

"Listen," she said, unable to contain how afraid she actually was of this man, "I'm married. I met someone, I fell in love, and I married him. I'm not the same person you thought I was. I wasn't ever, not really."

"But you were. Admit it. Admit it, and we're halfway there."

"Halfway where?"

"I know you. Only I know you."

"Don't say that. Please don't say that, and please, please leave me alone."

"Leave you alone?" he asked, then leaned close to her while she looked at him and then looked away. "Why, Louise, I never, ever recall you asking me to leave you alone before. In fact, I remember the words as being quite different."

"You're wrong. You're sick."

"Not really. Different, maybe, but not sick. But I'm honest about what I am, and you're not. And I hate that. I hate a fraud. I am what I am," he whispered, "but what is it you've pretended to be? What is it? Women like you make me laugh. You rut around in your inflamed heat, and then you pretend it never happened."

"Stop."

"Don't leave just yet. I'm not through. I'm almost through, but not quite, because I want the truth here. I want you to admit how much you liked it. You see, I know women, and I know women love what I do to them. For them. It's a gift, in a way. I love what you do for me, they say. They close their eyes as they do whatever it is I want, because, you see, it's what they want. They do it to themselves, and then sometimes, like you, they sneak away suddenly and pretend it never happened, pretend they are pure and proper, but then sometimes they come back, and they say just do it, just do anything you want, just don't ask me, just don't ask me if I want to or not, just do it, they say. Right, Louise?"

"I despise you."

"What are you afraid of? That maybe your husband will find out about us? He might. He could."

"Are you going to leave me alone?" she asked with the tears now brimming over.

"Actually, I don't care if I never see you again, now that I've told you what I think of you. I just wanted to understand the level of your denial, the level of your own self-deception."

"I'll call the police if you bother me again."

"And I'll send your husband a gift."

"He'd kill you. He'd break you in half."

"No, he wouldn't do that. I've seen men who find out their wives are not what they thought. After a while, if the story's a good one, they look like men who've had their guts cut out, or been neutered. They're never the same again."

"Walter would shoot you like a snake."

"I don't think so. More likely, he'd shoot himself, if I read all this correctly. That happens to sensitive, idealistic types."

"I hate you."

She pushed her chair back, got up, and, doing her best not to show her upset any more than it was already showing, walked quickly to her car with Rob at her side.

"Remember what you are," he said. "Remember what you really are. Next time you're in bed with your husband, think of me," he said and smirked and then turned away.

CHAPTER 29

W ALTER was at the shed attached to the small barn when Louise came back from work. He walked toward the house as she parked her car, and she started toward him.

The barn, which was the size of the average granary from the turn of the century, had sheds on both sides of it. Because this land could not support a dairy, and because, in the South, there was no need for indoor shelter for animals in the winter, except on rare particularly raw or snowy days, farms did not have the elaborate barns that were found in the North. The animals lived outside year round and usually had a shed or run-in they could get under when they'd had enough of rain or flies.

Now, as Louise approached the sheds, she saw they were full of red and yellow and green painted equipment and that there were two tractors, both green.

Walter explained what he'd bought. She barely heard what he was saying and barely saw all of what was in front of her. He wavered before her and his voice was distant and muted, and she only hoped her face did not betray her.

"That's a 430," he said. "The little one."

"Uh huh."

"The big one's the 2020."

"Oh."

"It's got a four-cylinder diesel. Lots of lugging power."

"Lugging power?" she asked, the words meaning nothing to her, nothing at all, considering what she was going through in her heart and how afraid she was that all of this was going to be tainted by this evil man from her past.

"Yeah, you know, low rpm pulling power."

"Right."

"That's a characteristic of diesels."

"The little one does it, too?"

She didn't care. She was trying to offer something because he was so excited.

"No. Not in the same way. It's a two-cylinder and lugs a different way."

"Neat," she said and smiled.

"You're not interested. You don't have to fake it, sweetheart."

"I am interested."

"You look like something's flattened you today. I saw it the minute you walked up."

"I did have a hard day."

"Again? See. This is not good. You shouldn't put yourself through that day after day."

"I know."

"It is your job, right? Not something else?"

"Right."

"You didn't see Mary today, did you?"

"No. Why?"

"Just wondering."

"Mary's good to me."

"She better be."

"Tell me some more about the tractors. What's that?"

"That's called changing the subject."

"Well, why not?"

"Because you're the one changing, and I want to know why."

"I'm really on edge, Walter. I don't want to talk about things right now."

"When?"

"Just not now," she said and raised her voice. "Later, how about it."

This was so out of character for her that Walter got as quiet and docile as if he'd received all the actual bad news itself then, as if whatever was affecting her had suddenly become real to him. He'd never seen her this way, no matter what had happened.

She went inside without apologizing. He remained outside with the equipment and tried to think how he should be when he went in to her.

When he did go inside, he failed to find her right away but then heard her talking on the phone in the bedroom with the door closed.

He went into the living room and plopped down in a chair. Beside the chair was another phone. Without having planned to and without thinking he would have ever done such a thing to his newly married partner and the love of his life, he slowly raised the receiver and listened.

Because he was quickly ashamed of himself, he quietly hung up the phone after he'd heard it was his sister to whom Louise was talking.

Soon Louise came into the living room and sat across from him and picked up a book and flipped through it. Smiley, who had followed her in, climbed up beside her on the couch. As she climbed up, she glanced at Walter, acknowledging both that she knew he wouldn't allow her on the furniture and that she knew she could do what she wanted when she was with Louise.

"You picked up the phone, didn't you?"

"Yes," he said.

"You shouldn't have done that."

"I know. I apologize."

"Who was I talking to?"

"Mary," he said. "It was who I thought it'd be, anyway."

"Well, she called me, if that matters."

"Oh."

"And what were we talking about? Did you listen long enough to hear?"

"Me, I guess. All I can imagine is that somehow I've messed up and she's your confidante."

"That's not it."

"Or else she's changed you in some way, and you have a life now I don't know about."

"That's absurd."

"That would be her way, to subvert you."

"You are so wrong about her."

"I know her well."

"And me. You're wrong about me. How could you be wrong about me?"

"I guess because I don't know what's going on, and if I don't know, then anything's possible."

"It's not to do with you."

"Work?"

"No. I wish you wouldn't push me about this. It'll make everything worse. I'm sure it will."

"Fine. I'll suffer in silence while you and my screwed-up sister work it out together."

"I don't want you to suffer."

"Is it something with her and not with you?"

"No. I mean, yes, she's part of it, but not directly."

"Oh, come on, Louise. You can't do this to me. I have to know. I'm your husband."

When he said *husband,* the word came back to her the way Rob had used it, and she was sad and furious to see how it was already tainted, how he had ruined it for her, for that moment.

"I can't tell you."

"You really can't?"

"I wish I could."

While she fed Smiley, whose patience was finally rewarded, Walter went into the bedroom to change out of the clothes he'd worn to load and unload the equipment. He threw the dirty clothes into the woven hamper Louise had brought from her apartment and put on a clean pair of slacks and a white shirt.

When he saw Louise go out to the sheds to look over the equipment, he knew she was doing that to have something to talk about with him, knew it was her kind heart that was at work again, knew she was trying to be interested in a bunch of sheet metal and cast iron for his sake, and so, because she was out there for him, when the phone rang, she did not hear it.

It was Mary, who almost successfully covered her surprise at Walter answering.

"What's the matter?" he said. "Did you have something else you'd thought of to talk about with Louise?"

"You know we've been talking?"

"I wish you'd tell me what's happening."

"Nothing. We're just pals is all."

"I know it's more. Louise has said it's more. She's as much as told me something awful's happened to her. Or you or both of you."

"Oh, really? She said that?"

"In so many words."

"Well, whatever. I just wanted to touch base one more time."

"Have you gotten her in some kind of trouble?"

"No, Walter, I have not."

"You have a history of making trouble for people."

"Thanks a lot."

"It's true."

"I make trouble mainly for myself. That's my trick."

"Maybe."

"We just talk. She talks to me about things."

"She talks to you and not me?"

"Some things you do that way."

"Like what things?"

"Like things."

"I think you're behind this."

"It's not you."

"So you do know what it is."

"Sort of."

"You've got to tell me."

"I can't."

"You owe it to me."

"I do?"

"For years of listening to you and rescuing you. How many times? How many years?"

"Yeah. I know, I know."

"I want you to think about what you said. Why would she have something you could know and I could not?"

"Husbands and wives don't need to know everything about the other person. It's best if they don't, actually."

"Think how you'd feel if you were me."

"It's not you!"

"Who's Rob?" he asked so suddenly Mary went silent on the other end.

"Where'd you hear that name?"

"Who is he?"

"Some guy, I guess. It is a man's name, right?"

"Don't do this to me, Mary. You've got to help me."

"Oh, Walter, you know I want to."

"I won't tell her you told."

"You swear?"

"I swear."

"Listen, what little I know is that some jerk she used to date has called her on the phone at work, or something."

"Called her? What do you mean?"

"Just called. He wanted to talk to her."

"Maybe he didn't know she was married."

"He knew."

"It's got to be more than that. You're not saying Louise thinks I would care about some ex-boyfriend, are you? I wouldn't."

"He's not a nice guy, let's say."

"Not nice like how?"

"Listen, Walter. I'm going to have to bail out here. I just am."

"If he's threatening her, I'll call the police in on it."

"No, don't do that."

"Why?"

"I think the threat involves something that would embarrass Louise."

"Then we'll make sure he doesn't carry it out."

"I think it involves you, to be precise. Like he's got something he could show you that you really wouldn't want to see, believe me. Like it's a kind of, well, video thing. Of Louise. And him."

The bottom did drop out of Walter's heart and guts then, just like Rob had said it would. His insides felt as if they had fallen out through his groin. He felt as weak and broken as if he had been hit in the stomach with a concrete block or sliced open from his throat to his belly.

"A video?"

Their house had narrow pine boards on the walls and ceiling. Although the trim was cut square, butt to butt, over the doorway and windows was an extra piece of molding. This extra piece was evidence that whoever built the house had wanted to go a step further and make it special, not grand, but different and a little nicer than it might have been without the additional detail.

Attached to one of the extra molding pieces was a nail from which hung a type of plastic doll that young girls had in abundance around their rooms and on their beds. Walter was looking at it when Louise returned from the barn.

"What do you have there, old fellow?" she asked.

"I don't know what you'd call it."

They each then knew more than either of them knew the other knew, and both of them were pretending as well as they could.

"It's a troll. I don't know why a troll doll would be something I'd keep, but I've had it for years."

"Oh."

Then neither of them seemed to be able to follow up with anything else to say. It was as if nothing was going to be able to fill what was between them but the truth itself.

"You know," Louise said, "oddly, we've switched places."

"How's that?"

"I walked in just as you were getting off the phone."

There was the opportunity, then, for one of them to simply open what was before them. It was something that would have to be done. They were stuck apart in the room facing each other, and there was no way for them to get any closer or to continue on with that day, if not with more to come, unless they talked about all of it.

"She called again."

"And you wanted to know what we'd talked about?" she asked.

"Yes."

"And she told you?"

"Not easily and not all of it, I'm sure."

"I wish she hadn't."

"You see, I'd heard the name Rob mentioned, so she had to take it from there."

"Oh."

"Do you really feel this man is a threat to you?"

"Yes, I do," she said.

"Then we'll do something about it," he said. "Me and you and Mary and whoever else we need, we'll do something about it."

"**I** KNOW YOU'RE SURPRISED to hear from me," Mary Pristine Calhoun said.

Sometimes people are asked to act with heroic sacrifice. Other times the heroism is simply unavoidable.

"So, how've you been?"

Suppose you saw a child fall into a lake and you swam out to save that child. The rescue would be a heroic act, but not a great one. Most people would do the same.

"So, what are you teaching this semester?"

But then suppose the water was ice cold and the person who fell in was an adult and the reason he or she had fallen in was because of something irresponsible he or she had done.

"That was a crazy night at the motel. I swear, it was wild. Weird, but wild."

Then only someone who had a reason would go in, and the heroism would be a cleansing and purifying act.

"I didn't get it then. I don't now. The more I've thought about it, though, the more I wish I'd acted different."

The rescuer may not enjoy what she's doing, but she will be changing herself in a way unexpected.

"I guess you are surprised. I'm glad you're pleased. A woman likes to please a man. Sometimes she forgets, and heck, Rob, it's the nineties. Can't a girl call a guy and tell him she wants to see him again? Can't she do that?"

Walter drove to his city house. The yard was clipped and clean. It made the house look less bizarre.

Next door he saw his old lawn mower stopped midway through cutting the front lawn. Behind the mower the cut grass lay even, but ahead of it the lawn had sprouted and died standing up.

He parked around the corner, facing away from his street so that if Manny came out he could be gone immediately. This made observing the house difficult and made him look suspicious. This method of waiting to catch Shirley alone was not going to work out easily.

It might not work out at all. He could have asked his tenants to discover when Manny was gone, or where he went or if Shirley was working, but that would bring them into something they had no business being part of and would lead to a curiosity that might expose his wife's awful predicament.

"It's better now," Louise was telling Nancy. "It's almost like I can't believe why I didn't understand how good he would be about all of it. Why didn't I know that? There's something wrong with me not to have known it, when he's been so good about everything else."

"He's rare."

"I know. Most of them are the Robert Wilmanses of the world."

"You're telling me."

"I hope that our meeting him ended all of it. Did you see how ugly he got?"

"He's scum."

"I mean, he was going on and on, and I didn't know what he was talking about after a while."

"Yeah. Strange, though," Nancy said. "I remember how that was what you liked about him at first."

"What?"

"That he talked."

"Oh."

"That he'd talk to you and listen to you, and you said it was something so new, it kind of swept you away."

"Yeah, well, that talking changed once things got further along. He had an agenda. He had a plan for me. I don't want to think about it."

"Did you see the new baby in neonatal?"

"Yes. He's darling."

"It's another under-three-pound miracle that's going to live, I think."

"We're getting those now. I wonder why there're so many premature births."

"The mother doesn't want him, either."

"I know. I heard. It's so sad."

"I'm so glad you're back," Nancy said. "And you may be right. He may just fade out now that he's had the chance to get ugly with you one more time. I doubt it, though, if you want to know the truth."

"At least I can work. At least I can concentrate enough to do that."

"We need you here. They need you."

"I felt so guilty leaving you the other day."

"Forget it. Tell me about the goats, and Smiley. And now you're into farming?"

Because Manny had not torn up the six-hundred-dollar check, he was able to cash it.

"I'm not thinking anything. I swear I'm not."

They had paid off their phone bill, as promised, and part of their electric and had had enough left over to have a good party. The money was gone now, and Manny was in between jobs.

"I was looking funny? I didn't mean to be."

A lot of men did not work as winter approached. This tradition dated back to the time of the hunter-gatherer, and then later the farmer. It was nature's way of letting the dominant male regenerate and prepare for the spring.

"Why don't I quit what? I don't understand. Tell me what you mean."

The men who were more in touch with their primitive selves had genetically mandated seasonal personas. This phenomenon was often not understood in much the same way that the symbols of the dominant male were misperceived in modern times, especially by women.

"But I wasn't. I never think about anyone but you. Never. What kind of look do you want me to have on my face?"

The state of dominance itself was burdensome, just as were, more primitively, the erectile and ejaculatory processes. Failing to understand this, modern women made demands that could cause a fellow to become annoyed.

"Do I want to do what? Sure. If you want to. I mean, I always want to. With you, I mean. Just with you, Manny. I meant it that way. I promise I did. Not with anyone else."

Manny wasn't acutely educated in the finer points of female desire and was one of those men who believed in the pound system of lovemaking. This had nothing to do with the British monetary setup and nothing to do with weights and measures but was closely related to the action of the compressor-driven jackhammer used on streets and sidewalks to break through the pavement.

"Ow. Slow down, would you, sweetheart? Just a little?"

Women who knew they had been bad or done wrong often responded well to unpleasant activities associated with intimacy, love, and passion. It was the duty of men to not let those women forget they had done wrong or been bad.

"Of course I like it. It's just that—"

Even if what they'd done wrong wasn't really wrong or hadn't actually occurred, something about the style of certain women attracted the men who would never let them forget it, whatever it was or wasn't.

"—I wasn't really . . . are you . . . oh."

Sometimes, in the middle or toward the end of the act, a thought crosses one or the other of the two people's minds. Sometimes, the man gets an idea or sees something or hears something or begins to make sense of something or remembers something, and this can ruin the moment. Why can't women learn to keep their minds shut?

"I'm sorry."

A man could, if he worked at it long enough and had the right gal, teach her to keep her mouth shut, except when it suited him to have it open. If a woman could just learn to keep her mind shut, as well, wouldn't it make her life that much easier?

"I'm sorry. I thought you were . . . oh . . . you weren't? I can try. I didn't. I did? I mean, gosh, Manny, I'm sorry. Don't be mad at me, because I will. I won't?"

At work, behind the counter at the wholesale electrical supply house where Vincent had been employed for many years and had almost accumulated enough time to retire and have his full pension, and where men, and then lately women, as well, asked for the male or female of this or that, according to how one part fit into the other—which had nothing to do with what was occurring at Shirley's house—and where the hum and drum of the day-long entrance and exit of the customers, mostly electrical contractors and building maintenance (pronounced there as "main-TAIN-ence") men, droned on like his fingertips rolling a rhythm on the Masonite countertop, he waited. He waited for it to be time to go home to see what there would be to eat, what there was in the paper he had missed earlier, to find out if Dorothy had heard from their daughter, and then to watch the news and snooze and rest and get his feet up on the highest setting of the retractable footrest in his recliner. He waited for this workday to be over, like so many more before it when he did his duty, earned the living, and put in the time that would, someday, allow all time to be his time, to do whatever it was he wanted, soon.

Manny left. Walter parked in his own driveway. He walked to Shirley's house. She was stunned to see him at her door.

"Why are you here?"

"I wanted to ask you something."

"But I was just thinking about you. I was just sitting here thinking I've got a few hours before Manny gets back and I need to call Walter or Mary or somebody."

"Really?"

"I got to get out of here. I got to leave now."

They walked behind his round house and sat on a bench.

"Maybe we can help each other, then," he said after she told him how bad things had been.

"You name it," she said. "You just name it."

He told her about his idea and why he needed her.

"I can do that. I can. But, listen, I'm going to need some money. I haven't forgotten I still owe you, but I'm going to need some more to get away."

"It's all right," he said.

"I want you to believe I'm serious this time. That I really am going to leave and stay away."

Walter only half cared whether she was serious or not. He didn't care about the money he would give her. He did care about getting into Rob Wilmans's apartment and how she could help him.

"I know you will," he said.

Mary Pristine opened her top buttons but then saw that without a bra she was too exposed, so she left only three undone and buttoned the fourth.

Of course she wore underwear. What kind of woman would go around without panties under a skirt, and a short one at that? A few years ago, when a man in Florida raped a woman, the judge dismissed the case because it was brought out by the man's defense attorney that she'd been wearing no panties at the time and a very short skirt, as well. The judge sided with the man because of the wanton nature of the woman.

Mary Pristine felt horrible. If she could have thrown up, she would have, she felt that sick at what she was about to do.

Shirley hadn't said much since she tossed her clothes into the trunk of Walter's car and carried out the few personal items she had to have with her, pictures of her daughter and things from her past, though not much else because there was not much else from her past. It had been lost or sold or left somewhere in another hurried move similar to this one.

She stared into her lap. Her hands were still. She was so quiet it worried Walter.

"You don't have to do any of this, you know."

"I want to."

"I'll take you back home. There's plenty of time before Manny gets back."

"Nothing ever works out for me. Nothing. But keep going," she said. "I want to do this."

"Come in, Rob. It's so good to see you. Do you want a drink? Don't even answer that because I sure do and I know you do."

Knowing women the way a few wise men did, Rob thought, allowed for the seductive and passionate quality of the woman to coexist with, how should one say, their often defalcatorial (archaic) manner; that is, should a woman, partway through the act of abandon, fail to follow through on her promise or deny a man the expectation created, there was a reason.

"You look great. Nice shirt. Wow. Is it silk? So is mine. It feels great against the skin. Neat hat, too. I guess you need a hat like that with the top down in cold weather."

The classic deerstalker hat was a style associated with certain literary works. It was constructed with a bill on the front and one exactly like it on the back and had earflaps that could be worn up or down.

"Great bow tie. I love it. It's so big. Have you been teaching? You came straight from teaching?"

Did you hear the story about the preacher that hard-working rural men used to tell? The hardest work, they'd tell each other, the preacher ever did was lifting a shot glass and a petticoat.

"You like the way I look? Well, thank you, sir. I tried to look nice for you."

The process of erecting was something women didn't fully understand. Having a flaccid body part containing cavernous tissue attain the respected form was something simple if what was transforming was only three-eighths of an inch in size and hidden from view.

"Tell me about your courses this semester. What are you teaching?"

Words, Rob thought, were important to a man's access to a woman's passion. A study of the literature, including readings in Erato, indicated that long conversations did even more than friction.

"Excuse my skirt. It's too short. I shouldn't have worn it. You like my legs? Thanks. I think if everything else goes out on me, my legs'll always be good."

Rational, creative dialogue and spending time with a man who enjoys matters of the intellect and has what might modestly be called a more refined taste than the average man, so to speak, was a relief to women, who were born with a paroxysmal duality of debased, uncontrollable desire and a purity that would inevitably fail them.

"You're so interesting. I'm sorry I was in a bad mood the last time we were together."

The thrusting reflex, along with other autonomic and primitive reflexive activity regulated by the hypothalamus, had been previously thought, the literature showed, to be more pronounced in the male. Lately, out of sync with any evolutionary explanation, the female had become possessed of a reflex of this nature that went beyond the male's.

"We could go to an early supper, if you're hungry, and then, I don't know, come back here?"

He was remembering a woman in her early twenties

(the older women were even more violent) who drove them both into the headboard of the bed. It made a fellow, jokingly so, to be sure, wish for the technology of automobile-style air bags around the bed, to keep from being injured by these women.

"Are you dating anyone particular now? Weren't you seeing someone just before me? Didn't you mention her to me some time ago?"

Walter and Shirley were in front of Rob's house. What had been the front yard was now the parking area. A strip of grass remained between the gravel spaces and the porch. A brick walk divided what remained of the yard. Grass sprouted between the bricks, and a screen was missing from one of the four tall windows facing the street.

"You wait here. I'll go up," Walter told Shirley.

"Be careful."

"I hate this," he said.

He entered the room with the key that Mary had given him that Rob had given her months ago. The sight of the man's room and his life and the pictures on the wall and his bed, unmade, and everything else that was there, including his and Louise's wedding announcement picture, sickened him, and he tried to find what he had to find without seeing all that he knew would remain in his memory no matter how much he hoped it wouldn't.

That Louise's face had been clear and unadulterated and pure in spirit, that it lacked the illusion of having been split into colorless silhouettes laid upon one another, as if tracing an outline but not getting it right, that she had this clarity and fine definition was something he was afraid might be lost. Now superimposed on Louise might be the images of this man and his room and his life and his greed.

The sadness of women that lived within them with the

same intensity as their delight and joy was because virtuousness and the lack of it both had a price.

The sadness of this day would not be easy for Walter to forget. It was the right thing to do, however, to never consider it again, to never see or think again about anything that was now before him in this room.

"I almost never eat that early," Mary said. "But isn't it strange that restaurants all over, or is it just in the South, open for dinner at five? It's something left over from long ago, I suppose. I wonder. I remember my grandmother taking me to the S&W Cafeteria when it was one of the nicest places to eat, and we'd always eat early. You know, you're not from the South, but it wasn't too long ago that we didn't have fancy restaurants all over every city. People ate at home. You rarely went out. This is all something new that came along with the Yankee invasion and mixed drinks."

She was talking all she could. The longer she could keep her mouth going, the longer it would be before anything else had to be going on.

"I ate light. So did you. Let's have some cake later on. I bought a pineapple upside-down cake the other day at the bakery down the street. I haven't had one in years, and I saw it and had to buy it. Of course, my mother would have made one. Why don't we cook like they did? Did your mother cook a lot?"

Did you even have a mother? she thought. Were you some form of genetic experiment? What was your father like? How is it that you ended up hating women so, because that's what it is, you know, behind all that finely tuned conversational folderol. You do hate us so very much.

"I'm so glad you were free tonight. You just don't

know how it made the evening work out so well. You just don't know. What's in that bag? Your books?"

Between his teeth were bits of green from the salad. His breath smelled like garlic. His fingernails, strangely enough for a man as fastidious as he, were bitten down. He wore no rings. His hands were soft, and there was almost no hair on them. The hair on his arms seemed to stop above his wrists, just above the visible wrist bone.

"Oh really? That's kind of interesting. Weird, but interesting. They have a magazine about that? Now where would a prim Southern gal like me ever have seen something like that, huh?"

His wrists kept disappearing as the French cuffs slid up and down while he gestured and talked. The cuff links were gold and looked to be simple round buttons with no adornment.

"Oh gosh, Rob. I don't know if I should look at it. You know I'm shy. Are you sure it's all right? I'm afraid you won't respect me if I look at it. Don't you respect me? I don't want to be bad. Please don't make me."

He was, in the face, quite handsome. Not knowing anything about this man, a woman might fancy him. He, like Walter in another way, was different from what women had to choose from in most men. He was handsome in a male model kind of way, and he was refined in his talk and his dress. A woman could take him home to meet her parents and not have to ask him to take a shower before he went. Later, she would be taking showers all day long to wash away the filth he'd left all over her.

"Don't laugh at me. You are, too. I can't help it if things like that make me blush. I am not playing with you. How about something to drink?"

Women were able to see in a man what he was like at birth. They could, if they needed to believe in him and in their love for him, or at least in their desire for him, see what he'd been on the day of his birth, the goodness and purity and innocence of his true character. This was an illusion most women were good at creating for a while, like a shaky work of art in progress. Then it failed. The smart women learned to stifle this urge to trick themselves the way they'd learned, early on, to sneeze with their mouths closed so that all anyone heard was a tiny *sssst*, while the unlucky women kept trying to paint the scene over and over, to fill in the numbers with the colors on the directions and have it make beautiful sense.

"All right. Okay. I'll do it. Don't leave. Don't be mad at me. I did say I wanted to have some fun. You're right. I did say that. Yes, I did."

"I got them," Walter said. "Let's go."

"Where now?"

"To a friend's house. To Mary's, actually."

"Oh."

"The money's under your seat. Go ahead and take it before we forget."

"Are you sure?"

"Take it. It means nothing to me. You need it. I'm glad to give it."

"But I haven't done anything yet."

"You will. Mary's lured this creep away so we could have access. We've got to rescue her. I need you now."

"All right."

"Rob, you are just so crazy! I swear you are! How can you look at that stuff? I can't do it. You are just too much, you wild man, you. Oh Lord, Rob, I'm just about to faint. I mean, hey, I'm for liberation and all that, but I just couldn't. I don't see how, I mean, those women, Rob, you've got to be kidding. I know you like my legs. I like them, too. You want to do that now? Well, I guess. Do what where? Like that? Wow. You are some kwazy wabbit. Did you hear the one about the Southern belle and why she hated group sex? It's because it took so long the next day to write all the thank-you notes.

"Somebody's here," Mary said. "I think I heard a car door. Did you? Maybe I didn't. I ought to go see. It'd be awful to have someone walk in and find us with our pants down, like they say. Now, big boy, you sit right there, and Mary's going to pull these back up and then this back down, just like that, see, and smooth the wrinkles out, see how we do it? Now I'm going to the door, and you put your brains back in your trousers, like a good boy. Somebody's out there. I can hear the neighbor's dog barking."

She opened the door and saw Shirley on the porch. Walter was out of sight in the car a couple of houses away.

"Yes?" she asked.

"Do you own a black cat?"

"Yes, I do."

"Your cat's been hit by a car. I'm from the APS, and we couldn't find a phone number for you, but we got your address from the tag. We've got her down at the vet's. She's going to need some work to splint her leg and some other things, and we need you to come down and authorize this and agree to pay the costs."

"Oh, hell. I'll be right there. Okay? Which vet? Where is it?" she asked, loud enough for Rob to hear. She talked a minute more before Shirley left, then returned to tell him she had to go.

"I know we could. I know it won't take long. I know, that, darling," she said, forgetting she could turn off the charm now. "But wouldn't it be better if we took our time?

I mean, don't you think it would and we got together some other day? I understand that. I mean, I know the research does say that about women. But honestly, let's wait, okay? I'll call you when I get back. You go home or get a drink somewhere, and I'll call you later. Please? Be a good boy, all right?"

Out in the car, Walter asked Shirley if she'd seen Rob, if his car was the one in front of the house.

"I don't know. Someone was there, but I didn't see him and I wouldn't know his car from a hole in the wall."

"I guess not. I don't know why I asked."

"Where are we going to go now?"

"Wherever you want me to take you," he said.

"I don't know. We never talked about that."

"How about a nice motel for the night. Or for the week, while you figure out if he's really going to leave your house. Give him a chance to get used to the idea that you're gone. How about that?"

"Okay. That'll work. I can call him and, if he's there, tell him it's over."

"But don't tell him where you're calling from. Promise me that?"

"I won't."

"This is your chance. Why be in trouble all your life? Why, Shirley? You're smart, you're attractive, you've got a lot of guts. You can do anything you want."

"I know."

"I think, if you want, you can get him thrown out of the house if he won't leave. You can do that, legally, I mean."

"He'll leave."

"Call us if he doesn't. We'll get him out of there."

"He won't cause trouble. Are we going to that motel?"

"Yes. Is that okay?"

"Sure, but wait while I check in. I don't want them to see me with all these grocery bags of clothes and stuff."

"I'll wait. We'll drive to your room after you get it."

She returned to the car shortly after she went into the office to rent the room.

"They want a credit card. I don't have one."

He gave her his card. After she came out of the office again, they unloaded the trunk.

"Call me and Louise tomorrow and let us know what you've decided."

"I will."

In one difficult day, Walter had, by the turn of circumstance, saved the life of one woman and saved the honor of another. Although it was only in the past few years that he had begun to understand women and, in understanding them, had begun, strangely, he often thought, to believe that something had gone wrong, that something unexpectedly made women more frail and vulnerable than before, it was peculiar that after this quiet day of minor, and, in the greater scheme of things, insignificant heroism, he did not feel particularly good or relieved or pleased or happy about what he'd done.

For Louise, his heroic act done with compassion and sorrow for the sad and unlucky things that happen to women, for Louise, at least, it was over.

Had he been certain that this man would not have gone to the police, he would have taken all the tapes he'd found under the bed. It broke his heart to see how one man could exploit the goodness and desire of so many women when their desire was something the women themselves did not understand. Predatory men sniffed along the trail of young, naive women until they found them, dined on them, and left them to whoever came along next.

If desire was still to be the undoing of women, and if

that desire still remained the domain of men because it gave men dominion over women, and if men now had this knowledge in a way they once did not, then the undiminished desire of women would forever be the burden of a man like Walter.

He stopped at a dumpster. He looked at the tapes for the first time since he had put them out of his sight. He looked at the handwriting on the boxes that said his wife's name, and he took the tapes from their jackets and studied them as if possibly something might happen by his looking at them long enough, as if he would think of something the way a good physician studies the face and eyes and color and manner of a patient, hoping for insight.

Wasn't it unsettling, Walter thought, how complicated and confusing the tantalizing nature of female passion remained, how it made it difficult for him to look away, how his feeling of wanting to punish a person remained, how the wordless, moody, sullen urge to hate oneself and everyone else could overpower good sense and the simple, enriching, and purely rewarding act of forgiveness.

He kept the tapes. He wrapped them in a section of a newspaper and put them in the trunk of his car.

GONADS SIN NO MORE

(John 8:11)

"IT'S SIMPLE, Louise. Give me a chance to explain it to you, okay?" Walter said.

It was February. Smiley was growing up.

"We have these goats. These goats are for meat. That's what we planned. The meat's going to go to people who need it. To get the meat from the goats, Louise, darling, you have to kill the goats first."

They'd had Christmas dinner with Vincent and Dorothy. Dorothy had been quiet and seemed, to her daughter, to be depressed. She denied it. Vincent had eaten a lot of food and had eaten it fast. Then he'd left the room.

"No one will slaughter them for us. The meat-packing plants around here won't do it, and the one up in the mountains that will doesn't give you back all the meat. They keep some of it for themselves, and you never know how much you should have gotten back."

Mary and Louise had become even better friends. This concerned Walter, though Mary seemed more calm and less desperate as part of the influence Louise had on almost everyone she was with.

"If we're going to do this right and be honest about it and provide this meat to the people who need it, and if no one will do it right but us, then, like everything else, it falls to us to figure out how to do it. Got it?"

Shirley had disappeared. Her neighbors reported that Manny had moved out soon after Shirley left and that sometime after that someone had come with Shirley and moved the rest of her things.

"If it falls to us to do it and if we are serious in following through on this idea, which is a good one, to farm this land and provide meat and vegetables and fruit and whatever else we can to people who need it, and if we want to do it economically and in a way that distances us from the corrupt outside world, right, which we have talked about and agreed is what we want, then we'll have to learn to kill them ourselves, and we'll have to learn how to do it in a better way than would be done in a slaughterhouse, which is horrifying for the animal and taints the meat with the fear of death."

In the hospital, at least in the emergency room, there was less to do in cool weather. Hot weather and long days and sleepless nights on sweat-drenched sheets or soggy, rancid bare mattresses caused men to want to hurt someone. It could be themselves they went after, or your sister, or your wife. Usually it was a woman. Men understood the lunatic mind better than women did and avoided crazed men. Women trusted that reason and goodwill would prevail in these situations. They were wrong.

"Since it seems that we're going to have to do it ourselves, and because you know I am anti-gun in all respects, then don't you think that we ought to find a more humane way to kill the goats, at least this one, as an experiment, so that the suffering would be as minor as possible? Huh? I mean, are you going to let me talk myself out before you say anything? Sweetheart? Tell me what you're thinking."

Louise heard his words, but she could not make her eyes break away from the wall where she was looking at nothing but horizontal boards. It felt so good staring like that and being unable to look away that she had not paid attention to everything he was saying.

"Are you daydreaming?" Walter asked.

"I don't want to do any of it," she said. "I don't want to kill the goats."

"Just one of them."

"But I will if that's what you think is right."

There. She had said it. It happened frequently that a woman would lose her sense of right and wrong and then, upon finding a man who clearly knew the difference, allow that she would follow him and do what he said.

"You agreed to all of this, didn't you? Am I not re-calling it correctly, sweetheart?"

"I did. You're right."

"What is it you're thinking about? Or who is it?" he asked.

She would let that go because she owed him so much and she loved him so much and it had been she who had broken the charm and innocence around them. She had been the one.

"No one. Not a soul on this earth. Just you, and I'm sorry I wasn't paying attention. Tell me again what the deal is."

"I don't want you to say things like that. I want you to understand why we're doing it before you agree."

"All right."

"Don't agree with me just to agree. There is a logic to this, and it's connected with how we've been discussing a way to remove ourselves from the corrupt world, or at least the way we've been a part of it up to now."

"I want to. I want to do that. You know I love you," she said, as if somehow all the words he'd been saying seemed to doubt she did and she felt she needed to reassure him. "And I'd do anything for us. Anything. It makes me happy to live this way, to live with you. Can't you believe that?"

Sometimes a husband would see his wife in a casual conversation with another man in a social setting, and her animation and lightheartedness and goofy antics during this casual conversation would actually cause him to feel bad because it would be clear to him that though she had been this way with him in the past, she was no longer as easily so. Something had changed.

"We can do it together, if it's the way you want to go. We can do it."

"The whole concept is so good. Maybe I'm not explaining it well. Excuse me if I've been clumsy about this. It's probably like everything else. The worst part of it is worrying about it, and then it gets easier as it goes on."

"Let's do it, then. Let's just do it and get it over with. I know you're right. It's the best way to do it," she said.

"The less we have to do with other people, the better off we'll be. The world is a great disappointment. I think we can do better."

"I know. I'm ready. If you want to do it, here I am."

In a few months Vincent would retire. Dorothy would then have to consider that her life as she had known it for so long would never be the same again.

He was not much use when it came to helping around the house, that is, within the house—cleaning up, sweeping, washing dishes, doing the laundry, cleaning the bathrooms. He was useful and willing outside the house and even enjoyed mowing the grass and trimming the hedges and getting up the leaves now that the gas-powered leaf blower had been invented.

She thought that if someone invented a broom that had

attached to the handle a loud gasoline engine that did nothing but roar and fume, then men like her husband would use the broom.

Because there had been a fight the night before about brooms and mops and cleaning, Dorothy was musing about all of this as she looked at the two pieces of the broom on the floor of the closet beside the sponge mop, the string mop, and the vacuum. The broom had been leaning against the breakfast-room wall when Vincent bumped into it. He then, to Dorothy's astonishment, kicked the handle so hard it broke in two.

This was unlike him, but it gave Dorothy a vision of life after retirement when he would be around the house with nothing to do and no one but her to blame for whatever it was he was feeling or hadn't forgiven her for, anything and everything, probably.

As she worried over this with another cup of coffee, trying to get herself going on a morning when she didn't feel like doing anything at all, Louise drove up. They talked, and Louise laughed at the broom story and eventually got her mother to laugh at it, too. By the time she left, Dorothy felt better.

She watched her daughter drive away. She envied her in a way that Louise did not know about. She envied what she saw as her daughter's freedom and ability to think and act independently, as well as the way she had found a man who adored her and talked to her and treated her with such affection.

She even envied how Louise had bought her own car and knew how to do such a thing, and what a loser she herself was in that she didn't. Her own car had twenty-three thousand miles on it and was four years old. It was a big car. Vincent had purchased it for her. He'd brought it home one afternoon. He had never even asked her what kind she wanted. If he asked her today, she still wouldn't be able to answer the question.

That she did not know how to answer that question or how to do so many things her own daughter could already do annoyed her.

She was glad, though, her daughter would not know the suffocation and confusion she'd once known. She was glad of that because it meant Louise would be free in a way she'd never been.

Mary Pristine was keeping the four-year-old daughter of a friend. The first thing the child did after her mother left was to stare at Mary's face and then get closer to study her even more.

"Have you been crying?" the child asked.

"No."

"Your face is red."

"I always look red-faced in the morning."

The girl's name was Jesse, but she had that moment changed it to Jessica.

"Your name is Jessica?"

"Yes, it is."

"I've always thought it was Jesse."

"No, it's Jessica."

"What's your middle name?"

"I don't have one."

"I thought it was Alexander."

"No."

The child had been talking since she arrived. She was looking at everything in the house and thinking so hard about all the things going on in her mind that Mary could almost see the thoughts forming and moving across her face.

"Are those my mother's shoes?" she asked, looking at the ones on Mary's feet.

"No, they're mine."

"I think they're my mother's."

"No, I promise you, Jessica, they're mine."

"Did my mother give you those shoes?"

"No. Maybe we both have the same kind."

"I have to stop the bottle today."

"You do?"

"My mother told me I have to stop it today."

"I didn't know you were still using a bottle."

"I do."

Mary was having a wonderful time. Taking care of the children in the nursery at church three or four times a year was fun, but having this girl to herself was making her feel good. She was smiling so brightly that if she'd looked in a mirror she might not have recognized herself.

"Do you think you'll be able to stop today?"

"I have to."

"Did you bring one with you?"

"No, I drink it at night."

"Oh."

Louise would soon have children. Nothing had been said about this, but she was the kind of woman who would want children and would enjoy them.

"Can we go outside?" the girl asked.

"Sure."

They found an anthill in the bare dirt beneath some pine needles. The anthill was built with fine red crumbs the ants had dug out of the red clay soil. The ants were going everywhere, in all directions.

"Let's see where they go," Mary said.

"Okay."

Some lines of ants were carrying food into the mound.

Others seemed to be carrying specks back out. Mary lay on her belly and propped her head in her hands and watched. Jessica did the same, imitating her exactly.

"There's one carrying a dead one," Mary said.

"How did it die?"

"I don't know."

"How long do ants live?"

"I'm not sure."

They lost sight of the ant with the dead body. They looked for it but couldn't find it. Mary was having more fun than she'd had in a long time.

"Let's kill one and see what they do," the little girl said.

"Okay."

"I'll smush one up, and let's see where they take it," she said.

"Okay. They must have a cemetery somewhere. We'll watch them have the funeral," Mary said.

A woman spending time with children could be herself with them in a way she could never be with a man.

"You're back already? I wish you had told me you were going to see Dorothy. I would've gone with you," Walter said.

"I didn't know I was going until I got on the road," Louise said.

"You didn't?"

"No. I thought I was going to get something for us to have for supper. Then I ended up going to Mom's, and now we still don't have anything special for supper. I forgot."

"We'll go out, then. I'll take you anywhere you want to go."

"That'll be nice."

"Are you ready to do, you know, the goat?"

"Are you?"

"As best I can be. I've got her in the shed. She hasn't eaten all day. It's best, I read, when you kill an animal for its digestive tract to be as clear as possible."

"Oh."

"It makes it easier to clean it, and for less contamination."

"Oh."

"They've been calling to each other. It's kind of sad."

"I know."

"Smiley's been taking turns keeping each of them company."

"She's such a good dog."

"After we kill it, we're supposed to let it drip out overnight, as long as we keep it cold."

"It's cold enough, isn't it?"

"Oh yeah. You don't want it to freeze, though."

"No. That wouldn't be good," she said. She was answering the questions and responding while being only half there. The other half of her mind was anywhere she could think to be rather than about to kill a goat.

"The more blood they drip clean, the better the meat is."

"I see."

"The books say, and everyone I talked to says, that really the best way to kill an animal is to slice its throat really deep, while you have it tied up, and let its heart pump the blood out. It gets it out more efficiently that way."

"That makes sense," she said, feeling even more awful than only thirty seconds before, when she'd thought she'd felt pretty bad already.

"We're not going to do that, though."

"Good."

"I think the animal is bound to suffer during that time, and the meat will be bruised and fouled by the suffering and thrashing about."

"Yes, I agree," she said. He was her husband. He was her hero. He had destroyed a bad thing from her past.

"A lot of times, people try to stun the animal with a sledgehammer."

"A sledgehammer," she repeated.

"But I've heard bad stories about missing and breaking off part of the skull or popping the eyes out or just having to end up beating the poor animal to death if you miss on that first crucial blow."

"Don't miss," she said. "Please don't miss."

"We're not doing it that way. We're going to drown the goat."

"We're going to drown the goat," she said. If he kept on talking then, she did not hear. She kept hearing the words *we're going to drown the goat*. She heard them so many times that eventually they came back out of her mouth once more. "We're going to drown the goat?"

"Yes. I figured out that was the most humane way."

"Please tell me you're not serious."

"I am."

"It's the most humane way?"

"I had a feeling you would say that. I had a feeling you would fail to see it."

"I do fail to see it."

"It's getting so I have to explain everything to you. But I don't mind. It's like this. From everything I've read, when people drown, they say it's the most peaceful death you can have. People who've almost drowned, or did drown and die and then came back to life, said they felt so peaceful and that there was no pain or fear, that they simply

202

relaxed and seemed to be drifting toward a bright light."

"It's not true," she said.

"Oh. I see. You know more than they do about it. I see. You know for sure it's not true. Listen, Louise. Why do you have to make something that's not going to be easy on me even harder? Why do you? After reading everything I could and thinking about it for days, I come up with this and you say I'm wrong after thinking about it for two seconds."

"Sweetheart, listen, I'll do whatever you want. I said I would. I'll help you any way I can. I've already agreed to that. But I promise you, I know what I'm talking about when I say that someone dying from lack of breath is not a peaceful way to go. In fact, it's probably the most horrible way to go you could imagine. I've seen it. I've seen it dozens and dozens of times."

"You haven't seen people drown."

"But I have. I've seen people drowning from the fluid in their lungs. I've seen it so often. It's worse than awful. It's nothing like peaceful. Walter, sweetheart, believe me on this one. The books may say that, but it cannot be."

"It's not the same thing. Evidently, it's not. There must be something different about the gradual accumulation of fluid in the lungs or whatever happens to people when they can't breathe due to the kind of distress you're talking about, and what it's like to suddenly be underwater and go out that way. I can't imagine anything else that would be easier, except if we gave the poor thing a shot of morphine. Can you get us that? And then wouldn't that foul the meat, with it flowing through the blood like it would have to?"

"Even that's not so good. You have to give morphine slowly to go out easily. There's no good way, Walter, but drowning the goat? Really? You believe this? Really, you do?"

"I do."

"Baby, listen to me. I think we need to get help on this. I don't understand why it's been such an obsession with you for us to do this alone. Why lately everything's been so much about doing everything ourselves. Let's just leave for a few hours and come back when someone we hire will have killed the poor thing and cut her up and bled her and whatever, and what we don't know won't hurt us. I mean, that's the best thing to do. It is."

"No. You're wrong. You're so wrong. You're so agreeably wrong. I want you to do this with me. I want you to do it with me and to do it today. I would like you to believe in me, if that's not asking so much. It certainly didn't used to be. I'd like it that my wife trusts me enough to believe that I wouldn't do something that was poorly thought out, or would be wrong. It's not often that I've done things that were wrong. I thought you understood that, and admired it about me. It's what you used to say."

"I do admire it. I do admire you."

"Then help me out with this and give it a chance."

"All right," she said. "I will."

"Don't do it if you don't want to. Do it because you can cut me enough slack to give me the benefit of the doubt that I might be right here."

"Absolutely. You might be right."

"Then let's do it."

"Okay. What's first?"

"I've got everything laid out over there."

"Good."

"I've got the knives, and I've got the vats to drip the blood into, and I've got the hand winch we bought to lift her up after she's dead, and then we'll slit her, and she'll drip all night into the vat."

"All right."

"Then tomorrow Murray's coming over to show us how to slice out the proper cuts."

"Okay."

"She's tied to the post, and near the post you can see I've put the round watering trough. She's been drinking out of it so she won't be afraid of it."

"All right."

"We're going to get her over the trough and hold her head down in the water until she expires."

"I'll try it," Louise said. "I sure will give it my best."

"According to what I've read, it takes about three minutes to lose consciousness and then about seven to completely die."

"That sounds right."

"I guess it is sort of your area of expertise. Is it right?"

"I'm not sure. Whatever you read about this particular way must be right."

They pushed the goat's head into the water. There was a lot of splashing and the dog started barking and they lost their grip and the goat raised its head and shook itself off.

"Put the dog inside," he told Louise. "She's not going to understand what's happening."

They put the goat's head under the water again. They held her by her ears and by her hair and by the knot of the back of her skull and mashed her down with all their weight and all the force they could. The goat thrashed around so hard and so violently that much of the water splashed out, but they held on until the goat again raised her head up and out of what remained of the water.

The goat's will to live was so strong it should have been obvious to anyone but Walter, who was determined to succeed, that if they had put the Empire State Building on top of the goat's head, she would have raised it up to get a breath. Nothing could hold her down. Nothing. Again and again they forced her under, and again and again she raised back up until finally Louise let her go. Soon afterwards, Walter did, too.

Louise was wet from top to bottom. Water dripped off of her face as if it had been she he'd been trying to kill. It took Walter a minute or so of catching his breath and drying his face and looking at Louise to realize that she was crying.

"It's not working. Something's not right. I know it's bad, Louise. I know this is hard on you. Let's try one more time, and then we'll stop. I think the problem is the legs. We've got to get her front legs knocked back out of the way."

She nodded. She didn't try to talk. She wouldn't have been able to. Had she opened her mouth, she would have sobbed, so she nodded.

"Let her relax. I'll get another rope. Stay with her. We'll just try one more thing. I hear the dog barking. Let me run inside to calm her down. I'll be right back."

The goat seemed to have forgotten what just happened and, what was worse, forgiven Louise for what she had been trying to do to her. She couldn't know that they were trying to kill her. All she knew was a mistake had been made and she couldn't breathe. She had to be able to breathe. As stupid as a goat was, she knew that.

People who have goats with horns are forever having to extricate them from fences. The horns grow up and curve backward toward the rear of the skull. If a goat tries to stick its head through a fence, the horns, like the prong on a fishhook, allow it to pass through. Then, when the goat pulls back, the horns catch on the wire, especially in woven wire fences. Then the goat might be there all day, pulling back and bleating and making everything worse with each passing minute.

People sometimes do that, too. Once they start on something that is wrong, they can't stop.

"She's okay," Walter told Louise, and put his hand on her shoulder and brushed her soggy hair out of her face. "She's been looking out the window at us. That's why she was barking. I put her in the back room. I'm going to tie these front legs together and then pull them out from under her and we'll push her down. We're not doing something right or it wouldn't be this hard on her," he said, tying the front legs together, which then caused the goat to flop over as if they'd been suddenly amputated. "Let's get her head under, and if it doesn't work, then we'll quit, I promise."

BECAUSE THERE WAS a thunderstorm and because Smiley hated the thunder and the lightning worse
than anything, she was frantically going from one hiding
place to another, to Louise, or under Walter's legs.

"What is it that you want me to do?" Louise asked.

"Concerning what?"

He had been reading the paper. The goat, in little packets, was in the freezer. Some of it had been difficult to
dispose of and was buried in a shallow grave at the edge
of the woods. The head was there. Lopped off and sitting
by itself on the edge of the empty hay wagon earlier, the
head had looked as if it wanted to be somewhere else, as
if it wanted to roll over and reattach to the body, as if it
might, unexpectedly, bleat sadly and mournfully.

"What is it you want me to say?" she asked.

"To do? To say? I don't get it."

No one in that household wished to try the fillet of
goat yet. It was going to be a long time before either one
of them would want to make a nice teriyaki sauce and stir-
fry some vegetables in with the little pieces of the animal
yet.

"You've got to tell me something. You can't just hang
me out like this and not tell me what it is that I've done

or said. Please don't do that to me. Please, darling," Louise said.

"Honestly, I don't know what you mean. Something's changed? I hadn't noticed. Tell me what it is. Have I changed? You mean the drowning-the-goat incident?"

"You know what I mean."

"Did I go too far? Yes, I did. I went too far. I'm sorry. I was wrong. I was so wrong."

The goat's tail, cut off and lying by itself at the other end of the wagon, was another one of those sights that would never leave Louise. That nervously flicking tail that had swung back and forth all day shooing off the flies, had lain there so miserably soaked and withered. Why had that man they hired cut off the tail?

"Please, Walter. Talk to me about what it is. I can't change if you don't tell me what the trouble is."

"Move," he said to the dog, then leaned down and comforted her after she rolled over on her back, assuming, rightly so, she'd done wrong by trying to get in his lap. "Just relax," he told the dog, and tickled her belly. "What trouble is it?" he asked, looking up to Louise.

"You've been strange with me for so long. Since before Christmas. You know you have. Are you tired of me? Is that it? Are you tired of me already?"

"Of course not. I adore you."

"Did we make a mistake? Did getting married change everything?"

There wouldn't be much to do with the gizzard of a goat, if it had one, which it doesn't, but for sure there's nothing to do with the intestines, the liver, the lungs, the kidneys, and the tiny convoluted brains, if a person took the trouble to crack open the skull and scoop them out.

"Not for me. Did something change for you?" he asked.

The raw heart of a goat is an unpoetic sight, and the smell is not good. On a day that starts out cold but then warms up in the brilliant deep blue sky of an unpolluted and brightly lit North Carolina winter day, a person might, glancing at the heart and taking a deep breath because it felt good to be alive, wish she were somewhere else.

"It all has to do with when you found out about Rob, doesn't it? I know it does."

"It could, whatever it is you're talking about. Of course, I don't know what that is, actually. I love you, darling. You know I do. Why not just move on?"

"Move on? Me? Oh, Walter. It's so mean of you to play this game. So mean."

"I would never be mean to you. Never. I want you to help me figure out whatever it is I can do to make you feel better. I want you to. I would hate for it to ever be said I'd treated you badly, as much as I love you."

"What happened that day I don't know about?"

The dog was whimpering and making such a nuisance of herself that Walter carried her outside.

"I'm going to put her in the barn," he said. "The last time we left her inside during a storm, she scratched up the bedroom door."

He put Smiley in a small room and tied a long rope to her so she could move around but not get out.

"She'll be okay," he told Louise. "She's in the room with the window high up. She can look out and see the stars, if they come out."

"What was it? I know how Mary got him over there. I know all that. What else? What did Shirley have to do with it? I never understood about that, and you wouldn't tell me, and I guess you told Mary not to tell me, or she didn't know, but was she just to be the person who tells Mary about the cat?"

"Come here," he said. "Sit beside me. It feels bad for us to fight like this."

"We're not fighting, sweetheart."

"It feels like one to me."

"I just want to know what's going on. I worry so much about us I don't do my job well."

"Some things are better left unsaid. This is true. Some things are best left to work themselves out, and the less said about them, the better," he said.

"I'm not sure about that."

"In this case, it's true."

"What happened? I have to know. I won't ever feel right until I know what happened that changed everything."

"You say it changed. I try to think that nothing changed."

"But you know it did," she said.

"But my effort has been to be the same with you. I've done it, haven't I?"

"Not really."

"Then I failed. Not you. It was me."

"Don't say that. That just confuses me. What happened?"

"Maybe I've been wrong about this, too, then. Maybe I have. Maybe I should talk about it."

She was shaking inside more than she'd been when she had to kill the goat. She was so afraid of what he would say.

"I got a key to his apartment from Mary. She had a key. She lured him away from the place so I could get in. I hated doing this. It made me sick. But it had to be done. Shirley went with me as part of the way we were going to rescue Mary from having to be with him any longer than she had to be. After everything worked out well, I took

Shirley to the Radisson, gave her some money, and left her there.

"I went to destroy the tapes, but then I didn't. I didn't do it, okay? I kept them. I didn't look at them, but I kept them. I put them in the trunk, and they stayed there and everything was fine, like you say, until just before Christmas, when I looked at them.

"I actually did it, I think, on a day when you were shopping for the new pickup truck you bought me. Isn't that awful? Isn't that, in retrospect, the worst thing about it, that you were buying me this fantastic pickup which I needed and wanted so much, and I was watching those tapes. I didn't know what you were doing, and I hadn't thought about the irony of it all until now, but that's the day that it happened, and I rue that day like no other in my life. I want you to know I still love you and nothing has changed except that, no matter how much I try, I can't stop seeing what I saw.

"So the only thing I can say is that when you see me going off somewhere or when things don't seem right and I'm not acting right with you or the way I should and certainly the way you deserve, then maybe a vision of something has taken me. I wish to God I had never done it.

"I wish to God you hadn't, either. I wish you had never met that man. You don't know how badly I've wanted to kill him, and I've never wanted to kill anyone in my life. But I have him. I've dreamed about taking a high-powered rifle and shooting him through the head, and that's me dreaming that, who doesn't believe in guns, and yet I do for him.

"I don't know what it was that made you be with this man and made you whatever it was you became with him, but I don't blame you as much as I do him. I know how men can be. I just don't understand why you would have gone so far with him. I despise the thought of you with him, but I don't fault you for it. I don't hate you for it.

"My keeping those tapes and looking at them shows about the same lack of good sense and the same bad luck that was in you, which is odd because I always thought of myself as having good sense and being reasonable.

"Had all this happened later, after you'd met Mary, I would've been sure it was her influence on you, but since it wasn't that way, I can't figure it out except maybe you needed to be something other than what I thought you were. Maybe you needed to do something wrong before you could be good, or maybe it's that this kind of man is what women really want, and this kind of degradation is what they really want, sometimes. I wonder if that's so, and if it is, then why? Why, I have asked myself, could this be true? I can't answer it, but I've seen my own sister become involved in the worst situations and attracted to men who appeared to me, when I met them, as close to pure evil as you can get, and yet, there she was, going at it, unstoppably.

"So I don't know. Sometimes, if you want me to be honest, I want to shake the living hell out of you, but I never would. But it gets to me how badly you've messed up and how things could've stayed perfect forever if this hadn't been. The disappointment of coming so close to something perfect and pure and then losing it because of you gets to me. It gets to me bad. I think young women are screwed up now. I don't know how to explain it. Just look at what could have been and now won't ever be. It will be wonderful, because it's us, but it won't be what it should have been, just because you had the bad luck to get mixed up with a man like that.

"So, yeah, I guess if you want to know does it make me crazy, then yes, it does. Doesn't it you? How do you live with it? Maybe that's the gift women have, that they can live with all of this or maybe it's only that I found out. Maybe it's that women like to think about this kind of thing in their past, because it is in their past, and that makes it all right, as long as they're being good now. What a rotten trick to play on a man if that's so. Now that does get to me, if that's the way it is. But how do you live with it? That's what I'd like to know. How do you?"

There was no answer she could give. The things he had said eliminated her ability not only to speak, to form words, but to even begin to form the language in her mind.

She left the room. It was evening. She thought she would never sleep. She thought, as she lay in their bed, that she would lie there all night, frozen and sleepless and tormented from forever having a night's sleep, but strangely, she did sleep.

When Louise awoke in the early morning, just as the sun came in the east windows of her sweet and safe cottage, she saw that Walter had been beside her all night and realized not only that she had not known he was there but that she had slept well. She remembered nothing until she thought about her dog out in the barn and quickly went to get her.

Before she got to the barn, she saw Smiley hanging from the rope her husband had tied her with. Her dog was hanging from the rope, and the rope went through the window back into the barn. She ran to her and picked her up to release the weight from the rope around her neck. She held her up with one hand while trying to untie the knot with the other, but Smiley was dead.

It looked as if the dog had made a valiant and considered decision to get herself out of the room and then had leaped out the window, thinking she was free. As she sailed toward the ground, the rope reached the end of its slack and hung her by the neck until she died.

How long had she been hanging there before she died? What must she have gone through before she finally died?

Louise carried her back to the house and sat with her on the same couch where she'd sat the night before and held the dog in her arms, waiting for her husband to see what had happened.

THERE WAS a meeting at the hospital where Louise worked. This meeting did not involve Louise. She was at work, three floors above the conference room.

"It is my opinion, and this is essentially a professional opinion, though it goes further," Dr. Mullet said, "that the release involve a better option with a more predictable outcome, a release to more stable environs."

Sue Mullet was wearing a business suit.

"I think the release of someone whose trauma has been not only so thorough but so openly documented has to be handled carefully and with wisdom."

The suit jacket was long. It came down to the midpoint of her hips. This was a good thing because she had put on so much weight that the zipper on the skirt beneath the suit coat would not pull up, not even an inch, and she had the skirt pinned closed at the top.

"I think, as the representative of the psychological community on this board, that I speak for most of my colleagues when I suggest that this option, which has been presented almost as a fait accompli, might I say, is neither a good one nor a healthy one."

The meeting was occurring one week after Louise had insisted that Walter tell her what was on his mind, and though a week had passed, no one, not even Mary Pristine, who could have been at this meeting but chose not to attend, knew what Louise was going through.

"Although I have no experience directly in this matter, as is the case with most professionals, since this type of case is rare, I have done some reading, and I think I can say that beyond the reading, my experience, as well as my intuition as well as my personal knowledge of a part of this option, makes it incumbent upon me to oppose it with the strongest recommendation against."

The group of people represented the ministry, the health field, the social services division, and the law enforcement sides of the dilemma. Social services held the cards. It was just Sue Mullet's bad luck that not only the head of social services in the city but the director of the department involved in this case were good friends of Mary Pristine's and had grown up with her and known her family. The medical doctor sitting on the board was a friend of her father's, as well. None of this was known to Dr. Mullet, who continued to make her case.

"I am going to speak somewhat off the record now, if that's all right, to tell you that although Ms. Calhoun was never actually a patient of mine, I did have occasion to have a long talk with her one day, and it is my impression that this is an unstable woman."

The head of social services and her assistant had to bite their tongues not only to keep from defending Mary Pristine but to keep from laughing themselves sick, knowing what they knew about Sue from friends and gossip and ex-patients and Mary herself.

"Furthermore, I am offering that, absent of any fee or reimbursement of any kind, but solely on the basis of goodwill and a curiosity into the matter, that I be allowed to have charge of the case and the ward thereof."

Right, Mary's friends on the panel thought. I bet.

A vote was taken after discussion had ended. It was decided, as had previously been recommended, that the gorgeous, sweet-natured, innocent and lost dear of a man, the amnesia man who had captured women's hearts with his sad, thrilling story months earlier, the man who was a blank slate and on whom a woman might want to write a script of life and love, Zephyry would be released into the care and handling of one Mary Pristine Calhoun.

CHAPTER 34

As MARY PRISTINE ascended, her sister-in-law declined, as one more unexpected revelation occurred.

"When you were three months old, I left home," Dorothy said. "I did it in a rage that had been working in me and I didn't know was there. The only thing I knew was I was going to kill someone if I didn't leave. I thought I might kill you or myself, but oddly, I never wanted to kill your father."

"You wanted to kill me?" Louise asked.

"I didn't want to. I felt like I might, though. It was just there in me, all the time. Actually, it wasn't a matter of thinking I might do something horrible; it was more that I was going to. I knew I was going to. I had something in me that was going to snap and I knew it and that wasn't like me, but there I was.

"So in one day, and I mean in one single, simple day's time during which no one on this earth knew I was about to run off, I packed my bags and put you to bed and I left, knowing, of course, your father would be home at five-fifteen, like he always was, and knowing that you would be safe, but at the same time knowing nothing at all or even caring, it seemed, whether you were or not.

"Please understand that I've got to tell you about it

because it seems, and I am only guessing, that something is working in you that is changing you, and I worry about it. I'm probably wrong, though, because it's through you and how happy you and Walter are that I've come to remember how unhappy I am. I'd forgotten. It's been so long since I thought about it, I'd forgotten how miserable I am. And yet, I'm also seeing that look on your face which I think was on mine."

"You are?"

"I'm maybe wrong. But I don't want you to do anything bad, and that's why I want to tell you about leaving you and what it was all about because you knew I'd been gone, even though I was only gone for seven months. You knew it. I could tell. You'd changed so much. Of course you had. A ten-month-old baby is nothing at all like a three-month-old, but it was more than that, and I hated myself for having done it to you and to Vincent, because I hurt him, too, I guess.

"I packed my bags and went out that door and left a note for your father and one for him to give to my mother, which was a harder note to write than the one to him because she'd done nothing wrong, and there's nothing easier when you're miserable and crazed than to blame your husband for everything that's wrong. But one's mother, on the other hand, if she's like Granny was, would never understand, and she didn't, but that's another story, the shame of all of that to her.

"Anyway, I was gone before five, but just before, so I guess I was making sure if you woke up, it wouldn't be long before your father was there, so I must have cared, although I recall that I was too crazy to care. I drove away in my own car and drove to Myrtle Beach to stay with a man."

Louise looked at her with even more surprise and mouthed quietly the question *who?*

"It was Uncle Alan. Right. You remember him. Not your real uncle, but your father's friend from the time he was in the army. It was him I went to because I had always loved him in some unspoken way, and I knew he had always loved me, and I was right because when I called him and told him I was coming to him, he let it happen. He let it happen like he'd known it was going to happen. He said every time he was around me, I looked at him longingly and like I wanted to talk to him but was afraid to, which was true. And he told me that he'd always felt sad to leave me when he went home, sad and lonely for me, which makes me want to cry now because at first, when we were together, I was happy and wildly in love like I'd never been, and the reason I'm telling you this is so you'll understand why I've been like I am all your life, because I know you must have wondered why I put up with things the way I have."

"I thought I knew."

"I can't ever do wrong again. That's something I learned about myself, how bad it is for me to do wrong and how much easier it is for me to live with whatever I have to, instead of doing wrong to someone. I learned that for me anyway. There was no hell like the hell I made for myself by doing wrong. Isn't that something? It's something I know people don't talk about anymore. They say please yourself and live your life to the fullest and all that malarkey, but they never tell you that for people like me living with having hurt someone and having done wrong is worse than anything else. For me, it was. Is.

"So for a lot of the first year of your life, I was gone and I didn't care. Most of the time I didn't. I was able to forget what I'd done for a few months, and I turned myself loose in a way that's not good. Not good for women, anyway, or for women like me, because we don't know how to stop. It's almost like we've got two speeds. Numb and dead and dutiful, or out of control. Those were my two speeds, anyway. But when I did think of you, how I did miss you. I don't think I can describe the day I came home and saw you for the first time in seven months. I can never make you understand what it was like to come home to you and your father except by way of saying the rest of my life was to clean it all back up, to never create another hell for myself to live through again. That's been my life. That's what I want to tell you. It worked. Doing good and doing whatever I had to do and doing right worked.

"So forgive me for having done that to you and then for having been such a pancake, such a doormat the rest of my life for you to see, but at the same time understand how it had to be. And understand, as well, I couldn't stop myself from going off with him. I couldn't. I've never been that way again and never was before, but at that time in my life, all I knew was that if I didn't leave, something worse than leaving might have happened."

HOW CLEAN was Mary's house that day? How clean was Mary herself? How many baths had she taken and then showers to improve on the bath?

Her phone hadn't stopped ringing. All her girlfriends were calling as the word spread from one to the other. The local news had heard about it, and she'd even had a visit from a syndicated TV magazine-show the day she brought Zephyry home.

She felt wilder and more full of that youthful expectation of infinite and heavenly happiness than when she'd been asked to go steady by the most sought-after boy in junior high school.

She was remembering the time she bought the bottle of ManTan that her parents hadn't known about. She and Sherry decided to put it on and then say they'd been out in the sun, only it was winter but it would make sense because they were in the eighth grade, and making no sense was the highest form of making sense there could be. The ManTan thing was cool, and everyone was talking about doing it.

Clay was about to ask her to go steady, but he hadn't yet. He'd bought the friendship ring with her initials put under the band, and she already knew about it, even though everyone was sworn to secrecy. Everything was going so wild, and ManTan was just another way of being wild and bad.

The day after she and Sherry put it on, something went wrong, and they looked like they'd been burned in a fire and had splotchy skin grafts all over their faces. Then Clay was embarrassed to be seen with her, and he didn't give her the ring because the ManTan had ruined everything. Even after it washed away and wore off, it seemed like nothing ever worked out again between her and Clay. Now Mary was remembering all of this and thinking about it because not much had gone right since that Sunday when the ManTan messed up her life.

Now she had Zephyry, and everything would be perfect, and the media was on the phone and everyone was curious about this new couple, and this man who was unlike any other man, and she hadn't even had time to tell her brother or Louise about him and about how she felt loving and wild and alive again.

She would drive out to their farm and be as happy as they were now. They could all be deliriously happy together.

Walter and Louise waited outside not for Mary but for Vincent, who had a surprise for them. Naturally, neither of them had told him about their own troubles, nor would they ever tell him, just as it was unlikely Louise would tell her husband about Dorothy's confession, feeling that privacy was needed to protect her mother as well as herself. She did not understand why this was, except that it seemed clear that husbands did not need to know everything. That was certainly clear now in a way it had never been before.

"Here he comes," Louise said.

Seeing the old man drive up nearly made everything feel normal. It would be her father who would be examined now, as it had always been, and not her.

"I wonder what he has for us."

"I don't know."

"I don't know, either."

"We'll find out."

"Yes, we will."

This was their new way of speaking. It was polite, and life, as it occurred each day, was discussed. Things were missing from the conversation. A lightheartedness had been lost. Louise considered it lost only temporarily. Laughter felt awkward and something she almost felt the need to apologize for.

"Whose car is that he's driving?"

"I don't know."

"Maybe it's not him?"

"It is. I guess they got a new car."

Vincent waved and then parked. The rear seat in the van was folded down. Something long was wrapped in a blanket.

"Dar hurt her hand helping me load this," he said. "She didn't feel like coming."

Louise looked at him now with all the knowledge she had of his past, what he'd been through, and all that had never been said. It had to be that she would never think about him in the same way again and that she, like her mother, should love him and allow him more than ever. Shouldn't she be that way?

"Is she all right?" Walter asked.

"She's fine. Just mashed it a little."

"Whose car is this?"

"It's hers."

"I bet she loves it," Walter said.

"I reckon."

Vincent unwrapped the grandfather clock, and Louise, having been raised to be a good Southern girl who now knew even better what that meant, exclaimed excitedly, though she thought its smeary walnut stain and cumbersome woodwork looked simply awful.

"Oh, Daddy! Is it for us? Really for us?"

"Yep. I've been working on it for months."

"Thank you, sir," Walter said.

"It works perfectly, too."

"Where's it been?" Louise asked, jumping up and down and meshing her fingers together like a child waiting for a birthday present, all the while watching herself and wondering how she was able to put on such an act for him. "In the attic or something? I haven't seen it in years."

"It was in the loft. In the garage."

The men carried it inside. Louise tripped running up the steps ahead of them to open the door, and the falter in her momentum almost broke her act, as well.

"You okay?" Walter asked.

"Heck yeah," she said and held the screen door wide.

"Where's your dog?" her father asked once he had set the clock down inside.

"She died, Daddy. She got sick and died," she added, hearing yet another lie come out of her mouth.

"Died? She seemed so healthy."

"We loved that dog," Walter said.

"I guess you can get a new one. You can always replace a dog."

They moved some furniture to make room for the clock. Louise got out a dustpan and broom to clean the floor where it would stand. Vincent motioned for Walter to come closer to him. He leaned in conspiratorially, and Walter knew what was coming.

"Have you ever had gas so bad it hurt?" he asked.

The statement, coming out of nowhere, plowing into all the heartache and despair they now knew in their lives, caused Walter to consider if this was the time to tell him that he didn't give a damn about his problems and nothing would suit him better than to never have a conversation about them again.

Looking at the old man's face, though, and seeing what seemed to be such loneliness and weakness there, Walter found himself going along with the game.

"I'm not sure."

"You better hope you don't. I feel like I got knives in my guts."

"You should see a doctor."

"They don't do no good."

Walter and Louise looked at each other, and both sensed how badly they needed to talk and how much they had missed each other since they last talked deeply and truly.

"I got in trouble the other day," Vincent continued as he noticed Louise leaving the room. "The old lady made me go shopping with her, and we were at the mall, and it come on me out of nowhere, and there wasn't no bathroom as far as the eye could see."

Walter nodded, then looked away as he thought he heard his wife going out the back door.

"Man, I held it and I held it. Sweat was just pouring off of me."

The back door closed again, and Louise walked past the doorway. She looked sad. Walter made a gesture of sympathy toward her with his hand, but she did not see it.

"I finally found the rest rooms, and I'm telling you, I made a mess in there. I feel sorry for the person what had to go in after me. You know what makes me mad? You know what?" he asked a second time when Walter didn't respond.

"What makes what?" Walter asked.

"The way they have to save money on toilet paper and the way they make it so thin, you know what I mean, that, you know, you got to use it, you get my meaning, and damn if your fingers just don't punch right through it."

Walter stormed off. After a minute, Vincent went to find him and saw that he and Louise were in the kitchen, holding each other.

"Now, now, this ain't the time for that," he said. "We got to move that clock back to the wall. And I got to show you how to work it."

"Show her," Walter said and left the house.

"Show her?" Vincent repeated. "Now what's wrong with him? Did I do something wrong?"

"Show me how, Daddy," she said. "Nobody's mad at you. Thank you for the clock. I love it. And so does Walter. Show me how to work it."

They heard one of the tractors fire up.

"I guess he's in charge of the farm and you're in charge of the house."

"That's it, Daddy. That's it."

After he left, Louise listened to the new sound in the house, the regular ticking of the clock. She watched the weights she would have to reset every eight days, and she knew that Walter would not be able to sleep with the sound of the ticking that loud, that he would hate the chiming of the bell at each hour and the single ring on the half hour. There it was, already going. No one wanted it, but there it was.

She watched him pulling the chisel plow with the larger tractor. At the end of each row, he pulled the hydraulic lever, and the sharpened points picked up in the air behind the big tires as he spun around and aimed down the next row so perfectly aligned that the earth behind the frame of the plow formed an identical match to the cut next to it.

It looked beautiful. The land changed texture and color and created a new pattern as the tractor went along slowly and steadily. Walter looked occupied and happy and relaxed.

He looked good. He was good. He had made a mistake. So had she. They had talked about it. They needed to talk more. Sometimes it seemed they would talk and then nothing happened.

She wanted to tell him that she was purely innocent in all of this mess but that he was not. The more she thought about it, it seemed he was not. She must have hurt him more than he'd hurt her. This must be true.

What had her father done to drive her mother away? Maybe it was just the overwhelming amount of nothing that he did for her and to her and with her. Who owed whom now, she wondered.

But the picture in the field was perfect for a moment. The tractor looked good, and the field rolling down from the house with the newly textured lines was charming, and wasn't that what their life was meant to be, charmed, like this scene framed in a moment of her reverie?

I could help him, she thought. I could say things that need to be said. I could help him, and we could be friends again. It appeared that he did not want her help anymore. He would rather be out there alone. In the past she would have ridden on the fender while he worked, and they would have talked about the noise of the engine. That now was gone.

As the time to feed the dog for the evening approached, she almost went to the kitchen to get the bowl and rinse it out and fill it up. Something was supposed to happen at this time each night, but not anymore. These changes had her acting as if she were about to fall off a cliff, either by saying the wrong thing or by doing the wrong thing or by merely having the wrong look on her face. The ease and comfort and simplicity and sweetness of their life had ceased.

So LOUISE continued to decline, while Mary ascended higher.

If there existed a heaven for women who lived for men, if there was a celestial resort for women who couldn't bear to be without a man, for women who adored the company of men, for women who only felt exhilarated when they were in love, then Mary had found a holy man and a divinity, and the other members of that religion could only wait at their windows and wish, knowing she had found such a man.

Like many people who become temporarily insane due to being madly in love, Mary did not see things in the way others who were not feeling that way saw them.

Riding in the car with Zephyry to show him off to Walter and Louise—Why wouldn't they be happy for her? Of course they would.—she did not realize how odd he looked in the passenger seat. He appeared as stiff and unreal as one of those artificial cardboard men that women sometimes bought to look like a real man on board so no one would bother them.

The poor guy didn't even know how to sit up in a car. After all, how could he? He hardly knew what a car was. Well, he knew, but he didn't know what he formerly knew about it. He could see what it was used for, but he didn't understand how to be in one. Mary would have to teach him this.

Teaching him everything was the thrill of it. Imagine being able to teach this man only what you thought he needed to know about the world, about other women, about you, and imagine that he would never doubt you or cross you or be anything but grateful to you. Imagine that all of him worked magnificently and that all of it was yours to play with. Pleasure was something that came from you and only you. Just think about it. That was what the gals had been thinking about when they wrote in to see if they could have a chance to own this fellow, and now Mary had him.

"Here he is!" Mary called out as she drove up. "Here we are!"

Mary hadn't looked so good in years.

"This is Zephyry, and this is my brother and his sweetheart of a wife and also my very dearest friend, Louise."

He shook Walter's hand and then he looked back to Mary and she nodded. He hugged Louise and smiled at both of them. He was happy. He was always happy except when he felt confused about something, or when there stirred something way in the back of his mind he could not get to. Then he looked worried, but he was never upset and he was never angry. What does it mean to be angry? At whom would one be angry? Why would that happen?

"Look at that field," Mary said. "Now you're farming, brother. Now you're doing it."

The lust is nice? Yes, I agree this lust is nice. But this lust is only for you, right? It does not happen otherwise? And this is not the same as love? It is unclear, but I want you to show me more about this lust, because I think I do not understand it the way you do, and you love the lust as much as love, or more than love?

"You're looking great, Louise. As for you, brother Walter, you're working too hard. Your eyes are tired. What are you doing to him?" she asked Louise. "Keeping him up late at night, you newlywed, you?"

Nonsense poured out of her mouth. It rained all over Louise like a beating, like a slow-motion flurry of punches, like being slapped numb.

"What a life you guys got out here. I'm thinking me and the boy might like a country scene. Now and then, anyway. Look at the sunset. Look at that color. My Lord, Louise, you could make a city girl go country."

The nonsense stung Louise like bees, like yellow jackets pouring out of the ground and swarming all over her while she stayed still and felt them slowly taking her down into the grass and covering her face and burrowing in her ears and crawling on her lips. Don't move. Be still. Don't talk. Think about something else.

"We can't stay long. I got Zephyry on a strict schedule. It's good that way. He knows what to expect when everything's the same each day. Don't you, big boy? He likes it that way."

Walter watched his happy sister and wondered what his parents thought. Since he had just found out, they likely either didn't know or had themselves just found out about the arrangement.

"Oh yeah, they know. I told them. Mom was speechless, but Dad was thoughtful and, you know, kind of guardedly pleasant about it, as if I was telling him that I was in love with a black man, but only a very light-skinned one. Kind of like that. Kind of frozen but hanging in there. Poor things," she said and laughed.

Pretty soon everyone was laughing. Mary was cackling

and Walter was laughing and Zephyry was chuckling and then laughing more as he patterned himself off of Mary. Louise joined in for a few moments, but it felt like she was going to laugh the tears right out of her eyes and the sobs started to build up in her throat so she began to cough and turned away.

"Take it easy there, gal. What've you done, caught something from that hospital? How do you stay so healthy and work there all day? You must be made of iron. What is it? Are you crying? What happened? Oh, the dog. I'm sorry. The dog. I haven't talked with you about her. I'm so sorry, and here I am strutting around like a fool and you still hurting so.

"Her dog died," she told Zephyry. "She was a beautiful dog. And so soft. Her fur was as soft as mink, I promise it was."

Louise went inside. Zephyry was touched and wanted to go with her and find out what this meant. He would have been the perfect person for Louise to talk to. He wouldn't have understood anything at all but would have been so sympathetic that she might have fallen in love with him had she not already decided she was in love with another man. Everyone knew being in love with two men at once was wrong, and she knew better than anyone that she did not ever want to be wrong again.

"What's up, bro? Is she, you know, with child? I mean, what's the scoop, boop? Give me the word, nerd. I mean, like, shoot me some illumination, is it all about procreation, or what could that have been about, her not being the kind to be down and out?"

Zephyry laughed again. Now it was again time to be happy. Was there something that just happened that wasn't happy? It was a blessing to be afflicted with the inability to remember what had happened and to only know what was going on right then.

"I'll call her. Tell her I'll call her. We've got to go. It's time for our nap, if you know what I mean," Mary said. "I got old Zephyry scheduled for three times a day," she added, and off they went, Zephyry sitting up in that car so proud and manly he almost looked real.

B ECAUSE Shirley wanted to save Walter from having any more trouble with Manny and because she was ashamed that she had gone back to him and because he had found what remained of the two thousand dollars and had insisted, in his own way, that she tell him where she got it, she told him it came from Rob Wilmans.

She told him that to get the money from Rob Wilmans, she had allowed him to videotape her doing it, and she made her story sound so real that even though not a word of it was true, Manny believed it and didn't like what he heard, not at all.

An act of retribution, then, grew out of the perversity and strangeness of Shirley's life. She waited down the street in the car while Manny hid in the bushes outside of Rob's house.

Those nunchucks really did their job. It was going to be a long time before Rob Wilmans ever enjoyed the pleasures of another woman.

"It's like it's gone," one of the doctors said.

"It looks like a bunch of red grapes someone ran over with a truck," another said.

"Yeah, you're right. Look at that little stem."

Shirley had thought that Manny would feel better and be nice to her once he came back to the car. She had hoped he would.

AFTER WORK on Monday, Louise went to see her mother. It was a good time to visit. Her father would not have come home yet and they could talk.

"You know, I'm remembering everything now. It's so odd. Now that you're married and settled and happy, things are coming back to me I haven't thought of in years."

"Really?" Louise asked. "I wonder if that's a common thing for mothers."

"I remembered what Granny told me when I married your father. I accepted it at the time and then, except for that time, lived it so thoroughly. She said you're married now. You belong to him. That is the way of marriage and women, she said."

"I can understand her saying that."

"It was almost exciting to hear it, to think about it. Thank the Lord you girls don't believe it anymore."

"No. That's a good thing. That we don't, I mean."

"I won't tell you all what Granny told me. I've already told you everything else and I've done you wrong, in a way, by being the way I was. Just don't mess up. Women can forgive everyone but themselves. That's what I've learned."

Louise nodded.

"Men don't forgive. They can't. It's just the way they are."

"It can't be for all men. Not really."

"I suppose it can't. But for most of them. For your father and his generation, that's for sure. They can live with anything, but they sure don't forget it."

"Men are different now," she said. "They understand us better."

"I hope so."

"They do. I'm sure of it."

They had hot tea with half-and-half and lots of sugar. It felt good. It felt rich and warm and comforting.

"It was odd to see Daddy after you'd talked to me. I was afraid I would be different. I tried not to be. I don't think I was, but I was worried about it."

"He wouldn't have known if you had been. He doesn't see anything but himself and what he's doing. He'd never notice it."

"I was thinking about Shirley a while ago. You know the woman I told you about?"

"Yes."

"I wonder what she did to make her like she was. Now I wonder that about everyone."

"Don't put me in the same boat as her, for goodness' sake," Dorothy said. "I haven't had such a bad life. You know that. We were happy. We were."

"I know. It's true. It's odd, though, knowing what I now know, that we were. That you were. That he was."

"Yes, it's odd."

"But we were happy, I guess, because you made sure we were. Right, Mother?"

"I tried. We all tried. Everybody tries in their own way."

"I love Walter so much."

"I know you do, darling."

"We're going to have a good life. Don't you think we are?"

"Of course."

"I'm not like Shirley, either," she said out of the blue.

"Why, dear, of course you're not. Where'd that come from?"

"Nowhere. I've been thinking too much lately, that's all."

The tea was good. It was decaffeinated. Being calm was important. Being still and quiet at times was important. Waiting and hoping was something women had done well for years.

BRER MANNY, he bin drinktin thim thar stuft wot tastid lak turpintime, and he dun gots him powerful angry.

"Evenin!" he sez. "Nice wedder dis evenin, aint it?"

Ole TarLady, she don say nuthin, she jist sit thar.

"I'z talktin tu yu," Brer Manny sez. "Aint yu gots no sinst ov reespict fur this hyar man?"

TarLady, she don say nuthin. She jist lay low.

"How cum yu don say nuthin. Iz yu def? Iz yu stoopid?"

TarLady, she caint say nuthin, she dun made sicht a turibul and bad misstak.

"If yu iz deaf, I kin holler louder," Brer Manny sez. "I kin jamd ma fist upsid yo haid."

TarLady, she dun gots reel steel. She aint movin.

"Yu iz one stuckup ladee," Brer Manny sez. "Yu no that? Yuz a runnin around with rich men agin, aint yu? Manny aint got enuf fur yu, iz that it?"

TarLady, she dun wisht so bad she hadnt made that fone call.

"I gwine tu sok yu frum hyar to hail war yu belong," Brer Manny sez. "Yu dun bin wid him agin win I tol yu not tu."

TarLady she caint say nuthin, she jist sit thar.

"I gwine tu larn yu tis timed, fur sure," Brer Manny sez.

Dats win ole Brer Manny drawed backt wid his fis and *blam* he strukt hur upt side der haid. TarLady, she don say nuthin, she jist sit thar.

"I'z gwine tu nok the natchul stuffin owtin yu," sez Brer Manny.

Then ole Brer Manny, he took his time, an bi-em-bi hyar cum anuthur big ole fist a blammin in tu hur. TarLady, she don't say nuthin, she jist sit thar.

"I'm axin yu fur the last timed, iz yu gwine tu spek tu me or iz yu aint?"

She jist sit thar then, cawz she dun wisht fur the cheeriats tu take hur away, cawz she dun fownded owt thit she watent evir gwine tu git away frum this hyar man at all, not nivir, and so she jist sit thar, not sayin nuthin, and hoptin to die wile ole Brer Manny, he dun got hissef so stucktid upt in hur they aint nuthin aylst tu du but kale hur.

An ole Unka Remus, he caint nivir gest how thangs dun chanjd down South, an the wa foks dun got thimsevz all mixt upt and stucktid tu ech uther, and the wa the womin fok dun fownd thimsevz in such a mess a venjurin owt into tha wurld all bi thimsevz and a darin the menfok tu cum and git it.

No sirree, ole Unka Remus aint nivir cud have gest how thangs have chanjd and how the poor ole womin fok dun fouwnd out thit Brer Fox and Brer Rabbit aint nun of thim gwine to be up tu no good. No siree, thim creejurs dun gots plum bumfuddled by the likes of thim womin a struttin thar stuff a jist astin fur it, aint no way to spute it, it be a najural fak, sho az yo born.

THE MONTH of March had passed. It would soon be time to harrow the plowed ground. With clay soils, the farmer had to wait until the land was completely dry on at least the top six or eight inches to harrow.

Pulling a disc harrow across wet, rough plowed clay produced not a seed bed but clods and clumps that hardened like pottery until the next winter when the freezing and thawing would break them up.

A farmer could plant seed in such a field, but not much would germinate and the harvest would be poor. If, however, he had the patience to leave the land alone until it was ready, and if he had done right by the land up until then, then what he would sow would bear well.

"Who were you looking at while we were eating?" Walter asked.

They had been to town and were back home before dark.

"Looking at where?"

"In the restaurant."

Walter was ready for spring. There was a lot of work to do, and Mary had volunteered Zephyry to help.

"I don't even know. I don't remember looking at anyone."

"You were staring past me. I turned around to see if it was someone we knew, but I couldn't recognize anyone. Who was it?"

"I don't remember. I must have been thinking about nothing and just drifting off."

"You were far off, that's for sure. It made me worry about you, darling."

Walter did worry about her these days. A particular vision from the videos worried him most of all.

"Don't worry about me. I'm absolutely fine."

"Maybe."

"But do make me aware of things like that. Really, do. I don't want to cause you worry about one single thing. Not one. I'll watch out for it from now on."

The vision that disturbed him most was of seeing her on the bed after all of whatever had just happened to her and with her was finished.

"It was probably nothing," he said.

She had, in that scene, looked as if she'd been washed onto the beach by the waves and then dragged out again, tossed up once more and then dragged out again and then again and again until she remained finally at rest on the sand, barely alive and so very still.

"It just seemed to me you were looking at someone or thinking something and weren't there with me."

"Oh, I was there. I'm with you. I am so with you."

Wasn't it odd that it was this image that stayed with him, and not an act of debasement or exuberance, but this vision of his wife having given herself until there was simply nothing left to give?

"If you say so," he said.

"I won't let it happen again. Thanks for pointing it out to me."

He opened the car door for her and held her hand as

they went onto the porch, unlocked the door, but then stayed outside looking across the fields.

"You know, men read things now and we learn things and all that, so I know women have an active fantasy life. I know that. We all know that now."

"I don't. I'm right here. I'm so grounded you wouldn't believe it. You ought to know that."

"It's disconcerting, though. To the man, I mean."

"Listen, sweetheart. Whatever it is you think I did, I won't ever do it again. I promise you that," she said.

"I'm trying to understand you, you know. I'm trying to be fair to you and allow that human nature is what it is."

"I'm yours, sweetie. That's all there is to say."

"You know I'd do anything for you. You know I have."

"Yes, you have. And I owe you. But listen, I owed you before that. I owed you because of how we loved each other, of how much I loved you. So nothing's changed. Not really. All right? Please?"

"Was it the man with the long brown hair?"

"Stop, would you? Just stop."

"If it was him, I guess I can see that."

"I can't take this," she said. "I just don't think I'm going to be able to take this if you're going to keep it up."

"He had that long, beautiful, well-combed female-looking hair you see on the romance novel covers. That's part of that female fantasy, right?"

She put her face in her hands.

"Did you want him? In some way?"

"Don't," she said. "Don't go any further."

"Did you want him in some way you don't want me? I think that's part of your makeup. I think it is," he said.

His voice was calm, his words were well-chosen, and he seemed to be asking a reasonable question. It was so much harder to recognize a beating when there was no blood and no bruises and no screaming and no slamming around. It was, at first, hard to believe that someone had been beaten so brutally.

"I don't want anybody," she said.

"If you'd wanted him, you should have told me. I'd have gone to his table and invited him to spend some time with you."

She began to cry. She kept her face in her hands, but the tears leaked down her palms and onto her dress.

"Don't cry, darling. I understand things better now than I did before. I knew a lot before. I think I can live with all of this. All that I know."

It had been a long time since they had made love. At first, it seemed it was the upset over Rob, then much later, it was the difficulty of getting back together, of breaking down the distance and the coldness.

"You know, at first I had this plan for us. Well, I mean, I've had lots of plans in my life, but I had particular plans for us, but that failed, I guess, and as you know I don't blame you, not really, for what happened. Things happen. Isn't that what is said? Things happen, and you move on."

She could barely hear him. She was almost deaf from grief and sadness.

"But then, thinking about all of this, I had another plan. I was curious what would happen. I thought maybe we'd do without for a time because I wanted to see what would happen, what kind of new way we would have with each other. Also, and don't take this the wrong way, but I wanted to see how long you'd last."

Had her puppy been alive, she would have been in her lap, climbing up to get to her face to kiss the tears away. It would have broken poor Smiley's heart to see her beloved Louise so sad.

"Not long, I see. But that's to be expected. Women, I think, live an eroticized life now that's unlike anything else they've ever been through. I've thought about that. Don't you agree? And knowing that and understanding it does change how a man would be with a woman."

The one remaining goat called from the bottom where it was too wet year round to plant and where the vines, now wrapped around the goat's head and horns, held it tight for a moment. The goat cried out and Walter looked toward it.

"You know, I didn't intend for this to be a mean thing. It evolved, more or less, as time went on and we began to be awkward with each other. But I think I did wrong, and I'm sorry. I was curious. After a while, I was just curious."

Louise had stopped crying. She was almost ready to take her hands from her face and look at her husband to see what he meant by all of this.

"The mean thing was, and I learned this and I'm sorry, was that a woman who loves the passion of being with a man doesn't do well denied that passion. It's different for a man," he said, and Louise looked at him then and saw how determined he was to carry this through, how positive he was about what he was saying.

"It's different for a man," he said, continuing on with the words as if the words themselves had the power to render neutral all that had happened. "Isn't that odd. A man might get angry. Take Manny, for instance. Or Mister Wilmans. Doctor Wilmans, I should say. I wonder what he does when denied. Don't tell me. Really, I don't want to know. But a woman begins to decline and then begins to make plans for another man.

"It's almost as if the desire and the passion, for a passionate woman, I mean—let's get that straight because there're so many more of you now than, say, in my dad's generation—but it's like the desire overwhelms you and you go toward it, like toward fresh air for someone who hasn't been breathing. Something like that. Am I off? Am I not right?" he asked.

She was even more wounded than ever, more confused and more helpless than ever. It was as if she'd sustained a form of brain damage that went beyond the skills of the medical arts.

"You know I do love you," he said. "I do love you, and I always will."

There was something about a woman whose tender heart and sweet, generous spirit so spilled over without bounds that softened all but the most cold-blooded of men.

Walter, then, loved her more at that moment than he'd known, and he was sorry for everything that had gone wrong, for what he'd done wrong, for causing her such sorrow, and for all that she'd done, as well.

"Let me kiss you, darling," he said. "Let's go inside and let me kiss you and hold you and let all of this be over. It's been so long since anything's been right. I just love you so," he said and led her to the bedroom and put her on the bed.

CHAPTER 41

ON THE STREET, in the evening, Rob Wilmans and his date encountered the sidewalk.

Around them were the cars and the buildings and the thin scrim of flaked skin as it sloughed off the sodomous lower orders of the population and settled on the ground beneath the polished black theater shoes of the couple.

Wilmans wore a cape black as Dracula's heart, and his walking stick was black ebony from a tree so hard and so remotely harvested that it had taken one very old native man all his life to cut it down, and carry it to the dealer.

Hatless, in a black tuxedo beneath the cape, Wilmans walked with a limp. It was a good thing he had the cane, because nothing else about this man was firm and never would be again, though the research did support that medical methods were available.

The research also supported that women would be there for this popinjay and his contemptuous, toplofty curiosa of erectile requirements.

"Zephyry, darling?"

He came trotting in so quickly and with such a trusting and hopeful look on his face, for a moment he almost looked like a young woman, the way women looked early on.

"We have to plan the rest of the day," Mary Pristine said.

He nodded and waited for the plan.

"And then, later, after we've had our nap, we'll go see my lovely sis, my sweet and true sister-in-law, because I love her, see, and I want to know what he's done to her."

Zephyry became serious, and was ready to stand beside Mary for whatever would be needed.

"Of course, I know he's done her in. I've seen it so many times. It was always me who seemed to be the crazy one. Did you know that?" Mary asked.

He didn't know, but there was no way it could be true. Crazy, he had learned, meant scary, dangerous, and sick. Mary be not of this.

"But I knew him, and I knew his women and I saw them and I watched, and I pretended he was pure because it seemed that he wanted to be. I gave him that, but it wasn't true."

Zephyry sat beside her on the couch. Her skin smelled good. Smells remained with him, and this was a smell he remembered as being good and happy, and he breathed it in, his lungs clear and deep as a canyon in the wilderness.

"I called him preacherman because he was so moral. But it wasn't moral what he did. It was never moral. His desire for goodness exceeded his abilities. Isn't that odd? It made him go wrong, and it was the women who always discovered it. I've discovered you, though, and now I know what goodness is."

Zephyry nodded and smiled. What a man he was. What a man.

CHAPTER

ONE AFTERNOON all the women in the family got together. They were celebrating.

"The house looks wonderful," Mrs. Perkins said to her happy daughter, Mary Pristine.

They were celebrating being women and having survived men and children and their own hearts all these years.

"Yes, it does look wonderful," all the other women said.

It was the first time since the wedding they'd all been together. This time, though, there were no men around.

"Well, you know, Zephyry loves to clean up," Mary said. "That boy just loves it."

They didn't know that they were celebrating having survived men or that they were glad no men were around that day. They loved their men too much to admit how much the presence of men would have changed things, except for Zephyry, who was more of a prototype, actually.

"I never minded cleaning house like some women do," Dorothy said and laughed at herself and what she was admitting. "I just never did."

Had the men been around, the women would never have been able to be this silly and this loose.

"I hate it," Mary said. "It makes me CRAZY!" she yelled, and they all fell over laughing.

Ever see two women driving along in a car, carrying on and laughing and accidentally running off the road and swerving back on, all the while tears streaming down their faces from the joy of it all? No men, you see, to keep them running in a straight line, to tell them when and how to shift or which way to turn to go the most efficient way.

"I guess I always had help," Mrs. Perkins said.

The days when a doctor was a doctor and there was no doubt about his authority were gone, as were the days when a man, any man, was a man with the power and certainty that went along with his gender.

"You could get a maid back then for five dollars a day," she said.

Those days were gone, too. Uncle Remus's great-great-granddaughter was now a senior vice-president at Pepsi, and you couldn't hire her for five dollars a minute.

"I love it all," Louise said. "I could clean all day long for that man of mine," she bragged. "I love my house, and I love my life so much I could cry."

"I haven't cried in years," Mrs. Perkins said. "Not from sadness, anyway."

"Me, neither," Dorothy said.

"My crying days are gone, too," Mary added.

"It's just seeing things in the right way," Louise said. "No matter what it is going on, you just have to see it in the right way."

"Ain't we just the happiest bunch of bunnies around?" Mary asked. "Ain't we, though?"

43

"LET'S DO SOMETHING wonderful," Walter said.

"Like what?"

"Let's have a baby," he said.

They were in bed. A week had passed since the women got together. It was the afternoon and the door was unlocked. If anyone had come to visit them, that person could have walked in and found them in bed in the middle of the day, and everyone would have been embarrassed.

"A baby?"

Had there been a dog in the house, this dog would have barked and let the two adults know that someone arrived. But there was no dog. The dog had died.

"You're always talking about adopting one of those premies in your care," he said.

The dog had died because she had been too spirited to be tied up and put away.

"You threaten to bring one of them home all the time," he said.

"Threaten?" she asked.

It was an odd word for him to use. The word ran itself through her mind again and again. It wouldn't stop.

"Well, whatever. But let's have one of our own," he said. "You'd be such a good mother."

Maybe she would have believed this a year ago. Now she wasn't sure, not only because of what her mother had told her but because she wasn't sure of anything like she used to be.

"I might be a good mother. Then again, I might not."

Outside, with the simple irrigation system Walter had installed, the crops thrived. It was a good thing to feed the needy when your own life was rich and full.

"It'll also make us closer," he said, "and I want that."

It was the right thing to do, and not many people did the right thing merely because it was the right thing, without any other reward. Only a saint would do that.

"Don't you want that?" he asked.

"I do. You know I do."

"You don't seem like it. Have I failed you in some way, once again?"

There was that confusing question he persisted in asking. It was confusing because it seemed she had failed him, or at least he said she had.

"Of course not."

Earlier in the day she had annoyed him when she served him a glass of milk with his sandwich. She knew better than that. He wanted iced tea with his sandwich in the afternoon, and if by chance they had sandwiches at night, then it was milk.

"Then let's do it," he said. "I do love you so."

It was hard to remember all the rules. There was so much else to think about and so many other mistakes yet to be made.

"I don't know," she said.

She almost said the word *no*. In her sentence was the sound of that word.

"You don't? How could you say that? We've talked about it so many times. What are you thinking?"

She must say yes. She knew she must. Because of how

badly things had suddenly gone in her life, she knew she must say yes to everything now, to be courageous and fearless and to make things right again, she knew she must.

"Yes, we have," she said.

"I've read about this. It's in the woman's nature to more than simply want a child. It's almost as if you won't ever be at rest or at peace or fulfilled without one. Isn't that what's said?"

"Maybe so."

"Maybe so?"

"I mean, yes, it's probably so."

"It's normal to be afraid. It's even wise. But you needn't fear anything about it. I'll take care of you, and I'll provide for you and our child forever. You know that."

That was true, she thought. He would.

"To give your husband a child is such a gift of yourself, and it's the gift to us, to our life, that only you can give."

It sounded right. There was nothing wrong with what he'd just said. It sounded like a good thing.

"And you know," he added, "and I don't mean this in a bad way to you, but simply as a fact, that the way women come into marriage now, with their lives and so forth, with their having a past, so to speak, there's not much left that they can give to their husband they haven't already given."

It was back to this, Louise thought. It was always back here, to where who had been given what was measured. It was likely she would be returned to this place and have it all measured again and again.

"But it's more than that. It's the way a woman actually gains power over the man and over her life that is played out through this gift. It's a gift to yourself, see?"

"Oh."

"On the other hand, you have the right to say no. You have the right to remain silent," he said and chuckled, hoping it would lighten the moment. "We don't have to do this. I will respect your decision."

"Thanks."

"I would respect it, though I would consider it poorly thought out and a bad mistake."

Please, God, she thought, don't let me make any more mistakes.

"So it's your call," he said, "although most assuredly it should be our call, although by whatever odd mechanisms have delivered mankind to this parapet on which we perch, it is your call."

Her skin went cold as she heard these words and the manner and cadence of his speech. The language froze her. It chilled her so thoroughly, she gathered herself into a ball and pulled the covers around her.

"All of these ideas and plans that people have for one another are known. It's not I who've created them. They are there. We are a part of them, and that's how it is."

She had heard this talk before, and it scared her to think that somehow she was back with another man like that.

"But I do want to give you a child, and I want you to give me one," he said. "And you know it's the right thing to do."

She had her eyes closed. She was trying to think. The words coming at her made it difficult for her to think. Leaving could be a mistake. Staying could be a mistake.

"Well," she said, "I certainly want to do the right thing. I always want to do that."

"Then don't worry so much," he said, beginning to unwrap her from herself the way one might uncoil a tangled rope, the way one would loosen a knot one strand at a time.

———

Down the road Mary's car was stopped at a red light. The traffic was sparse, but the signal remained red.

"I ought to run it," she said.

Zephyry was puzzled not only because Mary said that but because they'd left home just as what she called their "afternoon nap" was supposed to begin.

"Mary not want nap?"

"Mary want nap, but later. I got to see Louise. She's been too quiet lately, and I don't like that. I know my brother, and I know how he is, and I remember myself being that quiet, and it usually means trouble."

"Trouble?"

"Yeah, trouble. She was faking it at the party. I didn't say anything but I could tell."

IT WAS NOW thought that there had been a mistake in the transcription of something spoken many years ago. A well-known man speaking to a woman named Mary, but not our Mary, heard her story and then decreed that "gonads sin no more."

What was heard and what was written as law and truth was that Mary should "go and sin no more." From this mistake, many plans for the women had been created.

Because of all the plans, how could any woman begin again, and what would it be that she would begin? Could it be that knowledge had been what was missing and that with knowledge came liberation? Isn't that what was promised in the latest plan? The one the women themselves made?

Wasn't it promised that it would be different now, that pleasure would replace the foil packets of Miltown our mothers took and that the sad guilt of the accused nymphomaniacs would be expunged from their records and they would be free?

CHAPTER 45

BACK AT THE FARM that Walter had purchased for his wife and into which she'd arrived, hoping that her life would then begin in a way that was as important and good as her work, but even more so, Louise fought against the steady and deep and all-too-comforting and convincing voice of her husband as he held her in his arms and slowly broke her down.

"We're going to have a good life," he said.

She wanted not only to believe that, but to have it, which made his words hard to resist.

"You'll be happy. You'll be so happy, and you'll make me so happy."

What person on earth wouldn't want that to be true?

"Just give in to it, sweetie. It's so right."

She put her hand to his mouth and stopped the words, then put her other hand on his waist to hold him still.

"I hear something outside," she said.

He stopped. He sighed. He rolled off the bed and went toward the window.

"Like what?" he asked on the way. "What do you hear?"

"A car."

He was so quiet, then, looking out the window, that

she had to know what it was, and she asked if it was a car.

"It's them," he said. "Your sister-in-law and her mate."

"Wow," she said. "What timing."

"I'll say."

"Just stay there. Maybe I can get rid of them. Stay right where you are," he said and put on his clothes as they heard the door slam.

"We're here," Mary called as she and Zephyry entered.

"I see you are," Walter said and closed the door behind him.

"Yes, we are. America's favorite couple is here," she yelled back to Louise. "Me and the perfect man have come to show you the way."

"Keep it down, would you," Walter said. "She's sleeping."

"Sleeping? How come? Is she sick?"

"Just stay out of it. It's not a good time to visit, okay?"

"I'm not sleeping and I'm not sick," Louise said, while everyone turned around to see her coming out the bedroom door. "And in fact it is a good time to visit. A really good time."

Mary looked from Louise to Walter, who stared back at her but said nothing.

"Why so glum, chum?"

The women hugged each other while Walter stood nearby Zephyry. Walter looked old beside him. It was right he would look old. Zephyry was the new, improved model.

"Did your plan hit the fan, Mister Man?" Mary asked her brother.

The women were going to love this new model. It was almost like they'd created him themselves. It was almost like that.